"Will you consider marry

A Texas heartthrob, a man she'd been crushing on, was offering to make her his wife and help her get the green card she so urgently wanted. "If I agree to do this, there isn't going to be any intimacy. We can't..."

"Sleep together?" He roamed his gaze over her, up and down and all around. "I didn't think it would be an option."

"You didn't?" This was the most uncomfortable conversation she'd ever had. "I assumed that maybe you would..."

"Try to seduce you? I'm used to having affairs, so it crossed my mind. But you're different from anyone else I've ever been with. You just seem so—" he brought his hand to her face, skimming his knuckles along her cheek "—innocent, somehow."

For someone who wasn't supposed to be seducing her, he was doing a dandy job of it now.

* * *

A Convenient Texas Wedding is part of the Texas Cattleman's Club: The Impostor series—will the scandal of the century lead to love for these rich ranchers?

Dear Reader,

Sometimes writers take creative liberties with their books. Since *A Convenient Texas Wedding* is connected to other books in the Texas Cattleman's Club: The Impostor series and has a short time frame, I had to push some things along. In reality, I doubt anyone could get a green card as quickly as it happens in this whirlwind tale about an American millionaire playboy and his dreamy Irish bride. But then again, who knows? Maybe anything is possible in the fast-paced, internet-oriented world we live in today. Speaking of which, social media plays a big part in this story, too.

I love wedding- and marriage-themed books, and this one was no exception. Most of the story unfolds in a fascinating and fictitious Texas town called Royal. There were also some important scenes in Kenmare, Ireland—which is a very real place. I've never been to Ireland, but my research on Kenmare was fascinating. Someday I would love to go there. It's become my new dream vacation. But for now I was lucky enough to write about it.

Hugs and happiness,

Sheri WhiteFeather

SHERI WHITEFEATHER

A CONVENIENT TEXAS WEDDING

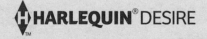

Special thanks and acknowledgment are given to Sheri WhiteFeather for her contribution to the Texas Cattleman's Club: The Impostor miniseries.

PLEASE RECYCLE · THIS PRODUCT IS RECYCLABLE ·

Recycling programs for this product may not exist in your area.

ISBN-13: 978-1-335-97136-4

A Convenient Texas Wedding

Copyright © 2018 by Harlequin Books S.A.

Printed in U.S.A.

www.Harlequin.com

Sheri WhiteFeather is an award-winning, bestselling author. She writes a variety of romance novels for Harlequin and is known for incorporating Native American elements into her stories. She has two grown children, who are tribally enrolled members of the Muscogee Creek Nation. She lives in California and enjoys shopping in vintage stores and visiting art galleries and museums. Sheri loves to hear from her readers at sheriwhitefeather.com.

Books by Sheri WhiteFeather

Harlequin Desire

Billionaire Brothers Club

Waking Up with the Boss
Single Mom, Billionaire Boss
Paper Wedding, Best Friend Bride

Sons of Country

Wrangling the Rich Rancher

Texas Cattleman's Club: The Impostor

A Convenient Texas Wedding

Visit her Author Profile page at Harlequin.com, or sheriwhitefeather.com, for more titles.

One

Allison Cartwright was in a pickle. The dill of all dills, she thought. The big, fat sour kind sold in American delicatessens, known for making one's face pucker. She might as well be making that expression right now.

Her temporary visa would be expiring soon, and she didn't want to return to her family's sheep farm in Kenmare, Ireland, bleating like a lost lamb.

Presently, she sat in the passenger seat of an Uber car. The driver had picked her up at her apartment in Dallas, Texas, and was taking her to the exclusive Bellamy resort in Royal, Texas.

On this hot summer afternoon, she'd donned a sleeveless blouse and a long, pleated skirt with side pockets. Her deep red hair was smooth and straight, and her fair skin was scrubbed clean. Although she'd gotten used to thinking of herself as more plain than pretty, she sometimes wondered what being the sophisticated type would be like. But she had plenty of other things, besides her lack of glamour, to occupy her mind.

As the vehicle advanced on the interstate highway that led to Royal, she glanced down at her cowgirl-style boots with their brown leather, blue stitching and pointed toes. She'd purchased them when she first arrived in Texas, and this was where she wanted to stay. Even as a child, she'd been consumed with America, most specifically Texas, studying about it every chance she got. She'd always dreamed of living here.

During her teenage years, she helped out on her family's farm and took online writing courses. Once she became an adult, she sold magazine articles to a variety of publications. But she also had a regular job, waiting tables in a popular tourist spot. She worked her tail off, saving practically everything she earned so she could visit the States one day and write an epic novel with a dashing Texas hero.

Then, just this year, she'd had an affair with the worst person imaginable, a handsome rancher and businessman who'd charmed her from the first moment he'd come into the restaurant. She'd followed him here to Texas with romantic notions and had spent three months growing closer to the man she'd known as Will Sanders. But that wasn't who he was. About a month ago, she'd learned that his real name was Rich Lowell. By then, he was gone, completely out of her life. But that was a complex situation, too. When they were still together, she'd been informed that he'd been killed in a plane crash.

The funeral had been horrific. But the kicker? The *real* Will Sanders had shown up, walking straight into the service and stunning everyone in attendance. Allison had been shocked beyond belief, particularly when she'd discovered the truth. At the time, she'd thought the man who'd died, the man with whom she'd had an affair, *was* Will Sanders.

The impostor had even stolen Will's face, altering his appearance to look just like him. Allison wasn't privy to the details of where Will had been during the nearly two years that Rich had taken over his life. But she'd been supplied with enough information to know that Will had been recovering from injuries Rich had inflicted upon him.

At this point, Rich was presumed dead. But while the case was still under investigation, the people who'd attended the funeral had been warned to keep what they knew among themselves. For however long it took to fit the pieces altogether, the authorities wanted Will to stay out of sight and "play" dead, as if there had only ever been one Will Sanders all along.

In some ways, Allison felt like a ghost, too, floating around with her pain. Fool that she was, she'd given the impostor her life savings, right along with a piece of her naive heart.

But she was venturing forward, one cautious step at a time. She'd received an anonymous note to meet with someone at 2:00 p.m. today at the statue of Diana in the gardens of The Bellamy. In part the note read: *I heard that your visa is set to expire. Do you want a green card? If you do, I have an interesting proposal for you. Yours, Mr. X.*

She had no idea who this Mr. X was or where he'd heard about her visa or what made him assume that she might want a green card. He could have come to her home since he obviously knew her address, having sent her the note. But he'd invited her to meet in a public place instead. She hoped that meant he wasn't a raving lunatic.

However, just in case, she was armed with a can of pepper spray in her right skirt pocket. Also, she figured that in an establishment like The Bellamy with security on staff, she could scream if he tried to accost her. Allison intended to be extra careful. Still, this was a risk, meeting a stranger and making herself vulnerable to him.

But damn it, she wanted a green card more than ever, especially after everything she'd been through. Forging ahead was a means of gaining her independence and restoring her self-worth, of not letting the man who'd broken her heart and stolen her money destroy what was left of her already fractured spirit.

Determined to stay strong, she glanced out the window, preparing for her meeting with Mr. X.

When she arrived at the hotel, she thanked the driver and exited the car. Making haste, she entered the lobby and checked her smartphone for the time. She had twenty minutes to spare.

She went over to the concierge and retrieved a map of the resort so she could make her way to the statue. The Bellamy sat on fifty-plus acres of lavish gardens. She wasn't going to wander the grounds without direction.

Thankfully, the marble statue was easy to find. As Allison crossed the lawn, she spotted it in the distance. Diana, the Roman goddess of the hunt, the moon, and nature, proved strong and beautiful, reaching for an arrow from her quiver.

But it wasn't only Diana that Allison saw. As she moved closer, she noticed a tall, striking man. He stood in front of the statue, with his stylishly messy black hair shining in the sun, and he was dressed in a button-down shirt and business tie. His shirtsleeves were rolled up, and with how powerful his aura was, he could've been daring the goddess to hand over one of her prized arrows to him.

Allison's breaths grew labored. He wasn't looking her way. His head was turned, his profile thrillingly familiar. Even from this range, she recognized him as Rand Gibson. He was closely associated with the real Will Sanders, and like Allison, he'd been at the funeral when all hell had broken loose.

Rand turned, all too suddenly, and appeared to catch sight of her from across the grass that separated them. She hoped that she didn't lose her footing and fall flat on her bum. Rand was a local celebrity of sorts, a much-talked-about millionaire playboy with a huge social media following. In her mind, he would make the quintessential book hero, the wild type who made women swoon. Even she had the maddest crush on him, and considering her latest ordeal, she shouldn't be having crushes on anyone.

In the real world, she barely knew Rand. Over the past month, since Will's funeral, they'd crossed paths a few times at the Texas Cattleman's Club here in Royal. Allison wasn't a member of the club. She'd been invited to go there by Megan Phillips, one of the other women who'd been hurt by Rich Lowell. But for now Allison was immersed in the mystery of Mr. X and how that was going to play out.

Rand couldn't be Mr. X, could he? No, she thought. It wasn't even two o'clock yet. Mr. X simply wasn't there yet. Besides, why would Rand offer to help her get a green card? And why would he send her an anonymous note? It didn't add up.

Yet, he seemed as if he were waiting for someone. Most likely he was there to rendezvous with one of his many lovers. Any moment now, a pleasure-seeking beauty was going to emerge from the other side of the garden and catwalk straight into his arms.

So what should Allison do? Keep heading toward the statue to wait for Mr. X? It was too late to hide behind a tree until Rand was gone. He'd already seen her.

If he knew she was there to meet a stranger, with a can of pepper spray in her skirt pocket, would he shake his head and tell her to go home? Not to Dallas, but back to Kenmare, where she belonged?

With the stubbornness associated with redheads, Allison lifted her chin and flicked back her hair. She wasn't going anywhere, except straight over to that damnable statue. When Mr. X arrived, she would have to lead him away from Rand, if Rand was still milling about. Of course Mr. X might stand her up altogether. She could very well be the butt of a joke. But that was a chance she was willing to take.

As she cut a determined path toward the marble goddess, Rand set out, too, striding, it seemed, in Allison's direction.

He moved at an easy pace, a flicker of a smile forming on his lips. Allison tossed a quick glance over her shoulder, making certain there wasn't another woman behind her that Rand was smiling at. Nope. She was the only female there. Saints preserve her, but maybe he *was* Mr. X.

They came face-to-face, and her heart stuttered in her chest. His electric-green eyes bore into hers. She had green eyes, too, the same noticeably bright shade as his. But on him, she thought the color looked far more intense. Everything about him was supernaturally gorgeous. He stood broad-shouldered and regal, with features consisting of darkly arched eyebrows, a straight, strongly formed nose and a prominent jaw peppered with perfectly defined, expertly trimmed beard stubble. But the final dream factor was his supremely kissable mouth. Insane as it was, she actually imagined taking long, luscious, forbidden tastes of him.

He said, "You're early."

She replied, "So are you." And now she knew,

without a shadow of a doubt, that he was the person who'd sent her the note.

He pulled a hand through his already ruffled hair. "I can tell you're surprised it was me."

She was still trying to comprehend it. She was also trying to stop from fixating on his mouth. She even had the weirdly carnal urge to run her tongue along the chiseled edge of his jawline.

"Why did you call yourself Mr. X?" she asked, wishing she wasn't having such bizarre thoughts about him.

"I heard that you're a writer, and I thought you might enjoy a bit of intrigue."

Allison only nodded. Besides being drawn to intrigue, being a freelance writer meant that she could travel and write from anywhere. Working in the States wasn't a problem for her.

Rand gestured to a small, ornately designed bench adjacent to the statue. "We can sit, if you'd like. Or we can walk through the garden and talk. I'm good either way, as long as we keep our conversation private."

"Let's sit." She didn't know if she could walk and talk and breathe at the same time, not while she was in his company, anyway.

They made their way to the bench and sat side by side. His big, muscular arm was just centimeters from hers. But with how cozy the bench was, it couldn't be helped. She should have chosen to stroll along the grounds instead, but she wasn't going to suggest that they pop up and start walking now.

"Before we get to the green card business, I want

to say that I'm sorry for what Rich Lowell did to you," he began. "He fooled so many of us. Me included. But I didn't see Rich all that much when he was impersonating Will. He spent more time in Dallas and abroad than he did in Royal."

She had to ask, "Do you think Rich is really dead? Or do you think there could be more to this than meets the eye?"

"I don't have all the facts, but I do know that the body was identified by a reliable source who assumed it was Will. So it sure seems as if he should be dead." He paused for a second and added, "Will told me that the FBI sent the ashes from the urn out for DNA testing. The results aren't in yet, but it's probably just routine. Or I hope it is."

Allison hoped so, too. "I hate that Rich used me the way he did. My heart still hurts from his betrayal, but giving him my life savings makes me feel like a total eejit." When Rand gave her a perplexed look, she quickly clarified, "Sorry. Irish slang. It means idiot."

He turned more fully toward her, angling his body on the bench. "I like the way you talk. Your brogue and whatnot." He playfully added, "Did you know that Irish accents were voted as one of the sexiest in the world?"

Her heart scurried inside her chest. He'd just spun their conversation on its axis, taking it to a flirtatious level. "Who would vote on such a thing?"

"Folks on the internet. I can't say I disagree. It is rather sexy."

So was the slightly Southern way in which he

talked. Not everyone in Texas sounded that way. He had a naughty twang that sent erotic ripples down her spine. Struggling to maintain her composure, she politely said, "I like your voice, too."

"That's good to know." He furrowed his brow, squinting in the sun. "With what I have in mind, we need to like things about each other."

Wondering what he meant, she waited for him to expound.

But instead, he asked, "Are you familiar with my position at Spark Energy Solutions?"

"I know that you were the second in command, and that Will was the CEO." She also knew that it was a highly successful oil and energy company owned by Will's family. "Initially, you worked under Will's direction, but you also worked for Rich when you thought he was Will. Then, just recently, you took over as CEO when Will supposedly died. And now you'll continue being the CEO until he can resume his life." She tilted her head. "But what does any of that have to do with me getting a green card?"

"I need a wife, Allison. Someone who can help me combat my image and provide what people think is a sense of stability. In the past, the board of directors let my reputation slide. But now that I'm heading up the company, the chairmen are pressuring me to get my act together. They're even threatening to fire me over it." He paused for a beat. "There's already enough uncertainty at work surrounding Will's stolen identity and how long it'll be before that gets resolved. The board can't afford any issues with me."

Allison could do no more than blink at him. Her mind had gone numb. "Are you suggesting that we marry?"

He nodded. "With the time constraints involved, we should do it as quickly as we can."

Again, she blinked at him. Rand Gibson was as far from husband material as a man could get. Not only was he a social media sensation, with tons of female followers hanging on his every word and sharing his pictures, his photos were sometimes made into sexy memes, garnering him even more attention.

Allison didn't follow him on social media because she didn't want him or anyone else to know that she found him so interesting. But she'd been poking around on his pages for longer than she cared to admit.

He continued, "At first people will be speculating as to whether a country girl like you can keep a playboy like me in line. But we'll make lots of public appearances and show them that you can."

She had no idea what keeping a playboy in line was like. She was already paying the price for dallying with a con man, and now she was being propositioned by a drop-dead gorgeous, modern-day Don Juan. The idea of getting close to Rand scared her senseless. He was everything she should be trying to avoid. Hot and seductive, she thought, and oozing with wealth and charm. Just like Rich when she'd first gotten to know him.

"How long would this marriage last?" she asked.

"It takes about three months to get the immigration

interview. I have a friend who works for the USCIS, so I can try to pull some strings and get it moved up. He can definitely get your security clearance done faster."

She wasn't surprised that someone as well-off and socially connected as Rand would know someone at the United States Citizenship and Immigration Services.

"We'll have to work out a prenup that's comfortable for both of us," he said. "I don't want things to get sticky later. But either way, after you get your green card and after I prove myself to the board, we can decide when we should split up. We'll part amicably. Then after the divorce, we can go our separate ways and no one will be the wiser."

"I'm not interested in a financial settlement, so a prenup wouldn't be a problem." Being dependent on Rand to replace what Rich had stolen wasn't the answer to restoring her self-worth. She would rather make her own way, even if she struggled to do it.

"So what do you think of my idea?" he asked.

She tried not to frown. "Of marrying you? What you're proposing is considered fraud. If immigration found out that we faked a marriage, there would be penalties involved. I suspect that your friend at the USCIS wouldn't appreciate you dragging him into a situation like that, either."

"I know, and that's why we couldn't tell anyone the truth, not even our friends or families. In order to make something like this work, we'd have to live the lie." Rand's expression turned dark. "The pressure the board of directors is putting on me isn't just to clean up my act. There's a company here in Royal that they expect me to bring in as a new client. And if I don't secure that account, I'll be ousted for sure. I've been trying to set up meetings with the other company, but their CEO hasn't responded to my calls. From what I've been told, he has concerns about my reputation, too."

"And you think having a wife will help?"

"It's the only solution I can think of that will improve my image in a quick and noticeable way." His expression grew even stormier. "You know what makes it worse? My father was always telling me that I was too much of a party animal to be taken seriously, that someday my behavior would come back to bite me in the butt. He criticized me every chance he got, even when I was a kid."

Allison considered how much information Rand was sharing. Rich used to confide in her, too. But all of his confessions were lies. She hoped Rand wasn't embellishing his tales to create a false sense of intimacy. Although she didn't doubt that he needed a wife, just how far would he go to get one?

"Where is your father now?" she asked.

"He died last year, but I've been feeling the brunt of his words more than ever now. I swear I can just hear him saying, 'I told you so,' along with everyone else who's convinced I'm not worthy of my job."

She couldn't hear anything but the frustration in his voice. "Are you sure that people will even believe that we're a true couple?"

"Granted, we'll be an unlikely match, but you know what they say about opposites attracting." He winked at her. "Especially if we show everyone how desperate we are for each other."

Allison's thoughts scrambled. Was their desperate union supposed to include sharing the same bed? Was that part of the plan of them seeming like a genuinely married couple? Just thinking about it was sending her into a tailspin.

She wanted to remain in the States, to defy the odds, to get her green card. But could she marry Rand? A man she didn't even know if she could trust?

Two

"Are you interested?" Rand asked. "Will you consider marrying me?"

Allison fidgeted in her seat. A Texas heartthrob, a man she'd been crushing on, was offering to make her his wife and help her get the green card she so urgently wanted. To some women, this would be a no-brainer. But it wasn't that simple. Not to her, anyway. And especially not if he tried to lure her into bed.

She said, "If I agree to do this, there isn't going to be any intimacy. We can't…"

He turned more fully toward her, one of his legs nearly bumping hers. "Sleep together?"

Her pulse jumped. "Yes."

He roamed his gaze over her. "I didn't think it would be an option."

"You didn't?" This was the most uncomfortable conversation she'd ever had. And the way he was checking her out with those wild green eyes was only making it worse. "I assumed that maybe you would…"

"I would what? Try to seduce you? I'm used to having affairs, so, yeah, it crossed my mind. But you're different from anyone else I've ever been with. You just seem so—" he brought his hand to her face, skimming his knuckles along her cheek "—innocent, somehow."

My goodness, my Guinness. For someone who wasn't supposed to be seducing her, he was doing a dandy job of it now. She couldn't think clearly, with the way he was touching her.

She forced herself to say, "You shouldn't be doing that."

He lowered his hand. "I shouldn't?"

"No." She didn't want her attraction to him distorting her common sense. "I still need to decide if I'm going to marry you."

"Well, are you?"

"It scares me, doing something so fraudulent." Trusting him scared her, too. But was she making too much of that? He wasn't a sociopath like Rich. He was just a man who needed to reform his image. His womanizing image, she reminded herself. He wasn't exactly an angel.

She didn't know what to do. If she married him for her green card, she would be committing a crime. If she didn't, she would be dragging her sorry arse back to Kenmare.

"I'd rather have an answer sooner than later," he said, "but you can sleep on it, if you think that'll help."

"It won't." She didn't want to think about sleeping on anything—or with anyone, for that matter.

"Then what's your decision?"

She considered her choices. Stay and regain her confidence? Or retreat and return to Ireland? Given her plight thus far, marrying him was beginning to seem like her only option. And at this point, she would rather take her chances with Rand than go home, lost and bleating, like the poor little lamb she kept comparing herself to.

She squeezed her eyes closed. A second later, she reopened them, just to say that she'd gone into this with her eyes wide-open. "I'll do it."

"You will?" He doubled-checked. "For sure?"

"Yes." She was going to take the plunge and become his newly minted bride, fulfilling her dream of living in the States, of working toward her independent future, of being her own woman. Starting now, she thought. Determined to show him that she wasn't a pushover, she reiterated, "I meant what I said before. The no-sex clause still applies."

"I understand. But we're still going to have to be affectionate with each other. We can't behave like strangers out there."

"Don't worry…" She paused, giving herself a moment to breathe a little deeper. "I'll play my part to the best of my ability." She would do what she had to do, short of tumbling into bed with him.

He smiled a bit too sexily. "At least there's no denying that we have chemistry."

In lieu of a response, she fought the warm, slippery feeling that came over her. But who *wouldn't* be magnetically drawn to Rand? Forbidden as he was, she could only imagine what climbing under the covers with him would be like. Hot and thrilling nights, she surmised, where she could let her inner sex kitten out.

Oh, sure. As if she actually had one of those. Even with as deeply as she'd fallen for Rich and his fake persona, she'd been a bit too restrained in his bed. She'd never thoroughly let loose with anyone, and this wasn't the time to start. She was absolutely, positively *not* sleeping with Rand.

"Allison?"

She started at the sound of his voice. "Yes?"

"We need to come up with a cover story about how we fell in love so quickly. But I have an idea about that."

"You do?" She cleared the erotic thoughts from her mind. "What is it?"

He waited until a passerby was out of earshot before he replied, "I thought we could say that we've been seeing each other behind closed doors. That I approached you privately after Will's funeral and we started to get to know each other then. With everything that's been going on this past month, I've been trying to keep a low profile and stay out of the limelight, so it's actually the perfect time for me to say that I've been in a secret relationship."

"That should work." Clearly Rand had a gift for

storytelling. So did Allison, of course. Fiction was her forte. "But for the people who know that Will is still alive and that Rich swindled me, we'll have to tell a more detailed tale. We can still use the secret-dating ruse, but we'll also have to say that you helped me overcome the pain of what he did to me. Only that I didn't want to tell anyone that we were together for fear that they would judge me."

"That sounds believable to me. I can more or less say the same thing, but in reverse. I was worried that if people knew we got together so quickly, they might accuse me of taking advantage of you. But now that we're bursting at the seams and eager to marry before you're forced to leave the country, we can't keep it a secret any longer."

She marveled at their savvy. "I'm impressed with how easily we came up with an explanation." Within no time, they'd concocted a believable romantic backstory. "You want to hear something funny? When I was a teenager going to school dances and meeting local boys, I had daydreams about stealing away from Ireland and marrying an American man. I've been consumed with your country since I was a girl. I used to write poems to my fantasy husband, spilling my heart out to him."

He touched her hand, ever so lightly. "Maybe you can incorporate that into the green card interview. The more we reveal about ourselves, the more authenticity it will lend to our case."

Suddenly she was getting nervous again, overwhelmed that she'd actually agreed to marry him. "You don't think it will make me sound foolish?"

"No. Not at all. And I'm glad that you're already sharing personal information about yourself with me. We're both going to have to do a lot of that. We'll need to know each other from the inside out before we meet with Immigration and tackle that interview."

She anxiously admitted, "The most challenging part for me will be lying to my family, calling and telling them that I met the man of my dreams. But the truth would be worse. They would never approve of a ploy like this."

"My brother is going to be my biggest obstacle. It's going to take a miracle for him to believe I've given up my bachelor ways and am capable of being a loyal husband."

"I remember seeing him at Will's funeral." Although Rand and his brother didn't look that much alike, they had the same mesmerizing mouth and sculpted jaw, coming from the same handsome genes. "His name is Trey, isn't it?"

"Yeah, that's him. Aside from our maternal grandmother, he's the only family I have left. Our mother died a long time ago."

"I'm sorry." He seemed genuinely hurt that his ma was gone. She noticed the pain in his eyes. Had she misjudged him earlier when she suspected he'd been embellishing his confessions?

"How many immediate family members do you have?" he asked.

She concentrated on his question. "I've got my parents, one set of grandparents and a brother who owns a media company that's headquartered in London. He divides his time between England and Ireland. Farming will always be in his blood. The Cartwrights have been in Kenmare for six generations."

"Is your father a traditional man?"

"Yes, he is. Angus is his name, and he adores me like no other. He fusses over Ma, too. As much as I hate to say this, he's going to be disappointed if you don't call him and ask for my hand in marriage. But I would never expect you to actually do it."

"Maybe I should, if it'll make things easier."

She nearly gaped at him. "Really, you'd appease my da?"

He glanced at a giant oak towering nearby. "I'd rather appease him than have him think that you're marrying a guy who doesn't respect his values."

"That's a good point." She followed his line of sight to the tree, becoming aware of the tangled shoots creeping up its massive trunk. "He and Ma have specific ideas about marriage. They have opinions about *everything*. I love them dearly, of course, but sometimes they still treat me like a child. Ma is especially good at meddling."

"My family rarely sticks their nose in my business. My dad did, but I wouldn't call what he did meddling. With him, it was more like bullying."

She felt badly for what he'd endured. Her parents wouldn't dream of bullying her. Everything they did was out of tenderness and care.

"Does your father Skype?" he asked. "Maybe I

can video chat with him to ask for his blessing to marry you."

"Yes, he uses Skype. Ma does, too. So she will probably nose in on your talk with him and want to meet you, too. But before you contact them, I'll have to call them and pave the way. They're going to be stunned by my hasty marriage plans."

"We're going to shock everyone." He paused, seeming reflective for a moment. "Do you still have the poems you wrote to your fantasy husband? Did you keep them?"

"No." She was feeling reflective, too. "But sometimes I wish I would have. I've always been a fanciful girl. Too fanciful, I suppose."

He searched her gaze, as if he was looking for something in her character that he'd missed, something he hadn't seen before. Then, in a near whisper, he said, "I think we should kiss."

She started. "I'm sorry. What?"

"Kiss." He repeated, his tone a little huskier, a little more seductive. "We're going to have to get used to kissing. We'll be expected to do it at the wedding, at the very least."

He was right. But with the penetrating look he was giving her, she was getting downright dizzy. She even gripped the underside of the bench, latching on to it with all her might. "You want to do it right now?"

He moved closer. "Now is as good a time as any."

She filled her lungs with as much oxygen as she could get, preparing herself, trying to stay calm. He leaned into her, and her heart boomeranged to her throat, before it zoomed back to her chest.

Staying calm wasn't possible.

As soon as his lips touched hers, she closed her eyes and asked the heavens to protect her. He invoked a carnal yearning in her, a spell he obviously knew how to cast.

He was good at this.

So very good.

An expert in every way.

The tip of his tongue teased hers, and she moaned like the sinner, the soon-to-be fake bride she'd agreed to become.

He cupped the back of her head and drew her even closer. He played with her hair, splaying his big masculine fingers through it, and she imagined making down and dirty love with him. The sex she refused to have.

Allison knew she was in for a rocky awakening, being tied to this wickedly delicious man. She tightened her hold on the bench. Only now she was using it to stop herself from putting her hands where they didn't belong. If one little kiss could affect her this way, she was going to have to fight to keep from mauling him—every desperate day that she was his wife.

Rand wanted to push his tongue deeper into her mouth, to nibble, to bite, gobble Allison right up, but he was holding back, trying to keep their arrangement in perspective. She tasted wholesomely, sensuously sweet, like honey straight from the jar. In his hungry mind, it could've been oozing down their bodies in warm, sticky rivulets.

Before his zipper turned tight and he got unbearably hard, he opened his eyes and eased away from her. It was going to be hell restraining his libido around her. But she'd implemented that no-sex clause, and he had no choice except to abide by it. Rand needed a wife to clean up his image and try to save his job, but he knew better than to take advantage of Allison. He probably could've gotten one of his high-society lovers to agree to marry him, but he'd chosen Allison instead. And not just because he assumed that she might want a green card. Her sweet nature was part of it, too. He thought that marrying a good girl would help his cause.

Her eyes fluttered open, and he stared at her. Even with the way she'd moaned, with the soft murmurs she'd made, she still struck him as innocent. One tantalizing lip-lock wasn't going to change his opinion of her.

She was still the same woman who'd been hurt by Rich Lowell, who'd been heartlessly used by him. He didn't know what that bastard had said or done to con her out of her life savings. To Rand, those circumstances weren't clear. But this wasn't the time to ask.

She peeled her fingers away from the underside of the bench, and he realized that she'd been holding on to it the entire time their mouths had been fused together.

"We did it," he said. "Our first kiss." He figured

that talking about it was better than sitting there in awkward silence.

She seemed to agree. She quickly replied, "Where I come from, kissing is sometimes called shifting. We also say 'the shift' or 'to get the shift.'"

"So I just got the shift?" he quipped, without really expecting her to answer. His gaze was still locked on to hers. He knew other green-eyed people, but he'd never met anyone whose eyes mirrored his in the way hers did. He sometimes got accused of wearing colored contact lenses to enhance his appearance. He doubted anyone would accuse her of that. Everything about her seemed genuine.

She blushed. "In some countries getting the shift refers to sex, but that's not how we Irish use it. To us, it's open-mouthed kissing, sort of like getting to first base."

"Where'd you learn about getting to first base?" Surely, Irish boys didn't say that when they scored with a girl.

"I picked up most of your slang from watching American movies. The romantic ones are my favorite."

"Chick flicks." He should have guessed as much. "You definitely seem like that type."

She studied him with those matching green eyes. "What inspired you to hatch this plan of yours? When did it occur to you that I might agree to marry you?"

"It was during the last Cattleman's Club event. I was standing off by myself, stewing about my job. You were there, too, and I overheard you talking to some friends of mine, saying that your visa was getting ready to expire. So later, I looked up your address online and sent you the Mr. X note."

"I was terribly nervous coming here to meet you," she confessed, reaching into her skirt pocket and removing a small black object.

He took a closer look and saw that it was a can of pepper spray with a key chain attached. "Was that to use on me?"

She nodded. "In case Mr. X was a nutcase, and he tried to accost me."

"Maybe I *am* a nutcase." Who else, besides a crazy man, would get married to reinvent himself?

"I think I'm one, too." She returned the pepper spray to her skirt. "So I guess we can be daft together." She referenced her other pocket, the one that didn't have the Mace. "I've got my ID, my money and a few other essentials tucked away in here. I didn't bring a purse because I wanted to keep my hands free to fight off Mr. X. I was prepared to scream, too, and alert security if need be."

"I'm sorry." He should have known better than to put her in a position that sparked fear. "I should have considered how meeting a stranger might affect you."

"Thank you. I appreciate you acknowledging that." She dug into her essentials pocket and produced a small tube, which turned out to be lip balm.

When she uncapped it and ran it across her lips, she did it so quickly and efficiently, he suspected that adding moisture to her mouth was a habit. Much too mesmerized, he watched her.

"This is probably going to sound strange," he said, "but is that honey flavored, by any chance?"

She snapped the cap back on, suddenly aware, it seemed, that his gaze was riveted to her newly waxed lips. "Yes, it is. But why do you ask?"

"Because I tasted it when we were kissing."

Her skin flushed, her rosy cheeks going rosier. "Should I stop using it?"

"Absolutely not. Use it as much as you want." He enjoyed knowing where the flavor had come from. "I liked it." Probably too much, he thought.

She put the lip balm away. "It's going to be difficult for me to kiss you in front of other people. I don't normally do things like that."

"I do it all the time. And if I don't get romantic with my wife when we're out and about, the gossip-mongers are going to say that I'm not as passionate about you as I've been about my other women. And we need to show them that I'm totally enamored with you."

She looked undecidedly at him. Clearly she didn't understand him any more than he understood her. They couldn't be more different from each other.

"Why have you been so public with your private life?" she asked.

"It started as a rebellion, my way of toying with society and thumbing my nose at my dad. And then, later, I just got used to doing socially unacceptable things and giving people something to gossip about. Of course, once social media hit the scene, I used that as my outlet. But at least I never made a sex tape or anything like that."

She all but blinked at him. "I should hope not."

With how primly she reacted, he got the sudden urge to tease her, to make things sound bawdier than they were. "Actually, it's possible I made a tape. There are a few blank periods of my life that I can't remember. But as far as I know, no tapes have surfaced. You haven't seen one with me in it, have you?"

"Goodness, no! I don't watch those." She crossed her arms over her ample breasts.

If she was trying to hide the fullness of her figure, it wasn't working. It only made him notice her delectable curves even more. Even in her loose-fitting outfit, a guy could tell what she had going on under there.

He continued his charade. "Are you sure you're not a sex tape connoisseur?"

"Yes, I—" She stopped and leveled him with an admonishing glare. "Are you mocking me? Is this a prank?"

He nearly cringed at the look she was giving him. "Sorry. I couldn't resist. With all the sordid stuff on the internet about me, I thought a sex tape seemed believable. But I guess I better not tick you off like this when we're married."

She sized him up again. "As long as you don't start talking like a cereal-box leprechaun or spout 'top of the morning' to me, I might be able to tolerate you."

Was she making a joke? He couldn't tell. Playing it safe, he said, "I'd never do anything that stupid." A second later, he saw her smile, and he knew he'd been had. He smiled, too, and they both laughed. He enjoyed the rapport they were building, strange as it was. Curious about her creative side, he asked, "What sorts of things do you write?"

"Magazine articles, lifestyle pieces, mostly for women's publications. But I've also been plotting a novel. It's about an Irish woman who goes to Texas and falls in love. I used to think that it should be a historical tale with the flavor of the Old West. But now that I'm here, seeing everything firsthand, I think a contemporary story might be the way to go. But no matter what time period I use, I want the hero to be the sort of fellow the heroine has to tame."

The way she was supposed to be taming him in this phony marriage? "That would never work on me, not for real."

"I know, but I think it does on some men, if they fall truly, madly in love. I'm a firm believer in destiny. I've always been a hopeless romantic." She rocked in her seat. "And I'm still trying to be. I don't want to lose that part of myself. Or miss the opportunity if the right man comes along."

Even after everything she'd been through with Rich, she still believed in love? He couldn't fathom it. Nonetheless, he said, "That's good, because I need a wife who projects that kind of image." Even if he didn't understand her propensity for love, he was glad it was going to play out in their favor. "Are you working on any projects now? Besides plotting the novel?"

"One of the publications I write for asked me to do a series of featured articles for them. I'm just waiting for the contracts to come through." Her expression turned taut. "I had to borrow from my parents to cover my expenses this month because of what Rich took from me."

He thought about the prenup she'd readily agreed to sign. "You made it clear that you're not interested in a financial settlement when this is over, but if you change your mind, we can still implement that."

"I won't change my mind. Being independent is important to me. It's everything, in fact. I don't want to be beholden to you, Rand. Not for money or anything else."

"Okay, but I'd still like to set you up with some credit cards while we're married. You can use them to shop or have lunch with other Texas Cattleman's Club wives or whatever society women typically do. But mostly you'll be with me. We'll need to be seen together as much as possible." He glanced down at her hands and how simply manicured her nails were. "I'll be getting you a big-ass diamond to wear, too."

She widened her eyes. "A big-arse diamond? I've never heard it put quite like that before."

"What can I say? I'm new at this fiancé stuff. But I think you should come home with me." Clarifying his intention, he added, "For us to get better acquainted and figure out the details of the wedding. If you're getting hungry, I can order some takeout and have it delivered."

"Thank you. That's a nice offer. I'm famished actually. I was too nervous to eat before I came here."

"Do you need a ride to my place? Or do you have a rental car with you?"

"I need a ride. I haven't driven in America yet. Being on the other side of the road confuses me. I've been taking Uber."

He stood and offered her his hand. "Ready to go?"

She allowed him to help her up. "Yes, thank you."

"You're welcome." He escorted her to valet parking so he could pick up his shiny red Porsche. To keep things fresh, Rand leased a different sports car every couple years. He went through women in a lot less time. In fact, he'd never stayed with anyone longer than a few restless months.

He glanced over at Allison. She seemed so foreign standing next to him. Not just the country she was from, but the knowledge, the hard-hitting reality of making her his wife. But if it worked out like it was supposed to, she would be reforming him in the public eye and on social media, too.

Of course he still had to be careful not to corrupt her with his man-whore ways. Even with the no-sex clause, he was pretty damned sure he could seduce her. Not that he was going to. As tantalizing as she was, he needed to keep his head on straight, to follow the rules. Trouble was, Rand was a rule breaker by nature. Restricting himself from the lust-driven pleasure of a woman's company wasn't something he'd ever had to do until now.

A young valet brought the car around, and Rand slipped the kid a generous tip. Once he and Allison were settled into their seats, he put the Porsche in gear and peeled out of the driveway.

As he headed for Pine Valley, the area where he lived, he asked her, "What should we order? What sort of food do you like?"

"I'm partial to the deep-dish pepperoni pizza you have here. I'm a hearty eater, just so you know. A bit of a pig, actually. I don't mess around where my meals are concerned."

Her candor amused him. She had a knack for admitting what some people would consider faults. "Your enthusiasm for food is refreshing."

"I'm glad you think so. Because it's something you're going to have to get used to."

He stole a glance at her lusciously curved body. "You can eat as much as you want around me." Trying to keep his errant thoughts off her voluptuous figure, he focused on the road.

A moment later, they engaged in chitchat. They revealed how old they were and when they were born. She was thirty-one, and he was thirty-seven. Interestingly enough, their birthdays were only a few days apart. They were both Aries. Normally he didn't follow that stuff. But she did, apparently, referring to their astrological sign as "hard-headed rams." He supposed that part was true, with as determined as they were to make this marriage situation work.

When he reached the entrance of Pine Valley, he stopped at the gate. He had a key code, but a live guard was on duty, too.

Once he moved forward, Allison glanced out her

window. "Wow! This is a grand area. Look at all the mansions. You live in one of these all by yourself?"

"Yep. Just me." Pine Valley was a private, upscale community with million-dollar homes, an 18-hole golf course, a fancy clubhouse and other exclusive amenities.

"You don't have a household staff?"

"I use a chef delivery service that comes by a few times a week and leaves my meals in the fridge or the freezer, based on the menus I choose. I use a cleaning service, too. I'd never have anyone live with me. I don't like having people under foot." He turned down his street and approached his home. The Tudor-style architecture featured heavy brick chimneys, decorative stonework, casement windows and a steeply pitched roof. An immaculate lawn dressed out the yard, with summer flowers garnishing the walkway.

He pulled the Porsche into his garage. His other car was a luxury sedan, another leased vehicle. Nothing was ever permanent in Rand's mind.

He gestured to the pearly white sedan. "You can drive that one when we're married."

"Thank you, but I'd rather not."

"Because of your discomfort about being on the opposite side of the road?" He didn't see why that should hold her back. "You plan on driving in the States eventually, don't you?"

"Yes, but I can wait until I'm ready."

Had she waited to have sex the first time, too? He suspected that she'd most likely lost her virginity when she was well into her twenties. He doubted that she'd given it up when she was a doe-eyed teen, writing poetry to her make-believe husband.

He escorted her into his house by way of the garage. They entered through the laundry room, with its high-efficiency washer and dryer, bright white counters and stainless steel sink.

Going from one spacious room to the next, he gave her a tour of the first floor, familiarizing her with the custom-built layout.

"Everything about your home is magnificent," she said.

"Thanks." He'd chosen furnishings that reflected his eclectic taste, mixing the old with the new, traditional with modern. "Let me get the pizza ordered, then I'll show you the rest of it." He called in the food and notified the guard at the gate, too.

While they waited for the delivery, he took her upstairs to where the bedrooms were.

They entered a room with an impressive view of the backyard. "When you move in, you can use this suite. It's the one my lovers use when they stay over. There's an adjoining bathroom with a shower and a claw-foot tub. Women seem to like that."

"It's all very elegant." She studied a gold-leafed dresser, tracing her hand along the wood. She turned and said, "But I hope you don't mind me asking, why do you have a separate suite for your lovers?"

He motioned to a set of ornate wooden doors. "This suite connects to mine, so when I have a woman over, we can open those doors and share both spaces. But we can close them when we want privacy, too.

In the old days, ladies had their own boudoirs, and I wanted to create that effect here, too. I think it's sexy, waiting on the other side for my lovers to be ready for me." He walked over to the canopy bed that would become hers. "Sometimes they come to my suite, and sometimes they invite me to sleep in this one with them."

She glanced at the pale beige material that draped the top and sides of the bed, then took a breath-stealing moment to look at him. He returned her gaze, steeped in his odd fascination with her. By now, she was standing in front of a Queen Anne–style vanity table, with her back to the beveled mirror. The wood was a deep, dark cherry, and the seat was upholstered in a light floral print.

Rand imagined her using the vanity on their wedding day. "Do you want to get married here?"

She widened her eyes. "In this suite?"

"No. In the house itself."

"Oh, yes, of course." She seemed embarrassed by her blunder. "That was silly of me."

"That's okay." He liked how unpretentious she was, how she didn't always behave accordingly. "Since we need to do this quickly, I think we should have a small, private civil ceremony. But it can still be traditional, if that's your preference."

"Something customary would be nice. I wish my family could be here, but they'd never be able to leave the farm on such short notice. Of course, they'll probably want us to have a second ceremony in Kenmare, in the church where I was baptized." She spoke softly, shakily, her voice hitching. "The second one would be called a convalidation, where our vows would be blessed and recognized by the church. But our marriage isn't going to last long enough for that. I would never do it, anyway. It be would be too sacred for a deception like ours."

"I know what a convalidation is. But to be honest, I haven't been to church in a really long time." It reminded him too much of his mother's funeral and how painful it had been to lose her. But he didn't want to talk about that. "I totally agree with you that a second ceremony is never going to happen. We just need to get through the first one."

"Yes, but don't be surprised if Da mentions us getting remarried in Ireland when you video chat with him."

"How about if I just go along with whatever he says for now?" Rand didn't want to upset her father. He'd been through enough turmoil with his own dad.

She remained with her back to the mirror. "That'll work. Just pretend you're on board with all of his ideas."

"How do you think your mother is going to react?"

"She cries easily, and me marrying my dream man is going to make her weepy."

"Right. The dream man thing." Never in a million years did he expect to be cast in that role. But here he was, trying to wear that mantle. "So I should prepare for tears when I meet her on Skype?"

"Most definitely. She's going to cry on the phone to me, too, when I first tell her about you. She's also going to offer to alter her wedding dress and send it to me. She always wanted me to get married in the same dress she wore when she married Da, and since she's a seamstress, she'll be able to do it right quick."

Rand winced. He didn't know anything about the process of handing down a dress, but it was obvious how important all this was going to be to her parents. "If you want, I can arrange to have your family attend the ceremony on Skype. We might as well make the most of that medium. Not just for me to meet them and ask for your hand in marriage, but for them to watch you become a bride."

"That would be wonderful. They would love that." She rewarded him with a wobbly smile. "Thank you for suggesting it."

"No problem." As he met her gaze, a stream of silence ensued. A soft, sweet, quiet heat, he thought, with his heady vibes mingling with hers. "We better go back downstairs for now. The food should be here soon. We can figure out the rest of the details while we eat."

She left her post at the vanity. "Yes, we should go."

When he moved away from the bed and turned to leave, she quickly followed. She even shut the door behind her a little too soundly, as if she was eager to close off the room.

And everything that went with it.

Three

Allison ate more than her fair share of the pizza. She drank the soda Rand had ordered, too. But in the center of her bride-to-be mind, her thoughts were racing.

She couldn't stop thinking about the boudoir Rand had built for his lovers—the sexy, dreamy, lavish suite where she would be staying. How she was going to survive sleeping there, she didn't know. Her crush on Rand was elevating to dangerous levels. Ever since she'd met him at The Bellamy, since he'd proposed this arrangement, since he'd kissed her with that scrumptious mouth of his, her pulse hadn't quit pounding. And now she was going to have to contend with his bedroom being intimately connected to hers, with two big, easy-to-open, elaborately carved doors between them.

"When are you going to call your parents?" he asked.

She glanced up from her plate, her arteries still thumping. "First thing tomorrow." She certainly couldn't call them today. It was later in Ireland than in Texas.

"I'll get your ring tomorrow, too. Maybe one of those sets where the engagement ring and the wedding band are designed to go together. I know someone who deals in antique jewelry, if older pieces are okay with you."

"Yes, of course." She wasn't going to interfere with his choices. "You can get whatever you think is best."

"The dealer works exclusively with a private clientele. She's a longtime friend of my grandmother's. I'll be inviting Grandma Lottie to the wedding, so you'll get to meet her. She's ninety years old and has a condo in a senior community here in Royal. It's a great place, as luxurious as it gets." He hesitated, reached for his soda, took a swig. A second later, he said, "But just so you know, her short-term memory is failing her. She has what's called mild cognitive impairment or MCI. Sometimes she forgets portions of conversations or repeats things we already talked about. I've gotten used to it now, but it was strange at first, trying to get a handle on it."

Allison couldn't imagine her granny going through something like that. Both of her grandparents were fit as fiddles. "Does MCI lead to Alzheimer's or other forms of dementia?"

"In some cases, it does. But her doctor doesn't

think that will happen to her. She has a caregiver who lives with her, so it helps to know she has someone with her all the time. Grandma Lottie was my rock when I was growing up. She stepped in when our mother got sick and raised us kids after Mom passed. I was ten at the time, and Trey was only four. He barely even remembers our mom."

"How sad for him. How sad for both of you." She didn't know what to say, except to express the grief she knew he was feeling. "But I'm glad your grandmother was there for you."

"Me, too. Without her, I don't know what we would have done. Our parents weren't even together when Mom died. They were already divorced. So by then, our father was used to being a weekend dad, to seeing us when it was convenient for him." Rand shook his head in obvious displeasure. "He never tried to take us away from Grandma Lottie, but he butted heads with her about what he called the 'indulgent' way she was rearing us. He didn't think she disciplined us enough."

"My parents coddled me. But maybe if I hadn't been so sheltered, I would have been more streetwise when it came to someone like Rich."

He narrowed his eyes. "I've been wondering about your relationship with him and how it unfolded."

"It's foolish, the way I let it happen." She picked at a piece of crust leftover on her plate, even if she'd been taught not to play with her food.

"Will you tell me about it?"

She winced. "Right now?"

He nodded. "Sorry, yes. But I'd really like to know."

She expelled an uneasy breath, preparing for the shameful truth. She'd already discussed this with the authorities and answered all of their probing questions, but repeating it to Rand seemed different somehow. "I met him at a restaurant where I was waitressing. I'd been working there for years, in addition to my freelance writing, so I could save extra money. Kenmare is a tourist destination, and we have lots of pubs and eateries." She picked at the crust again, tearing it into little pieces. "He said that he was on a much-needed holiday in Ireland, taking a break from his busy life. He explained that he was the CEO of an oil and energy company and how demanding his job was. He mentioned his family's cattle ranch, too, and his devotion to it. He was certainly my idea of a handsome Texan." She remembered how easily they'd talked and how forthcoming he seemed. "I thought he was as charming and interesting as a fellow could be. He took an immediate fancy to me, too. Or so I thought. But now I realize that he just saw me as an easy mark."

"Did you know he was married?"

"Yes. But he told me that he and Megan were getting divorced. That she'd met someone else and was in a secret relationship with that person. He also said that Megan was an emotionally fragile woman. According to him, she wasn't ready to talk to family and friends about the divorce or tell them that she was seeing someone else. She needed more time to get a handle on her new relationship."

"So Rich and Megan were keeping everything hush-hush? Gee, how convenient for him."

Her shame went bone-deep. Her foolishness. Her naïveté. "I shouldn't have fallen for a story like that. But he seemed so kind and sensitive, and I believed that he had Megan's best interest at heart. I didn't have a clue how often he'd been cheating on her or what a lovely and centered person she actually is." She released a sigh. "Of everyone I've met in Royal so far, she's been the most gracious to me. I feel so badly for her, marrying a man who wasn't even who he claimed to be."

After a long and silent pause, Rand asked, "When did your affair with him start?"

"Our romance budded right away, while he was still in Ireland. But I didn't tell my family about him. I knew they wouldn't approve of me seeing a married man, even if he was in the process of a divorce." She shook her head. "Or supposedly getting divorced or whatever." She continued her wretched story. "After he went home, we emailed and texted. He said that when I was ready to come to the States, he would help me get a visa."

"So you took him up on his offer?"

She nodded. "But he also said that he would try to help me get a green card, too, so I could move here for real."

"And make all of your Texas dreams come true?" He squinted at her. "Did he offer to marry you?"

"No." So far, Rand was the only man who'd ever proposed to her. "But his 'supposed' divorce from

Megan wasn't finalized, so that wasn't an option. Besides, our relationship was still really new. We wouldn't have been talking marriage, anyway."

"Then how was he going to help you get a green card?"

"He said that he knew some government officials who could probably make it happen." She paused, thinking back on what a tall tale it was. "It's strange because you're the one who actually knows someone who works for Immigration."

"Yeah, but my friend isn't going to just magically get you a green card. It doesn't work that way." Rand watched her with a curious expression. "How long were you together with him in Texas?"

"Overall? Before the plane crash? It was three months." Ninety days in Dallas, she thought, of being duped. "After what he did to me, after being conned by him, it makes me want my green card even more. I don't want him to be the cause of me losing my dream of living in the States."

He continued to watch her. Or scrutinize her. Or whatever he was doing. She glanced away, needing a reprieve.

He asked, "Did Rich know you had a savings account? Did you share that information with him?"

She returned her gaze to his. "Yes, I told him. But it never occurred to me that he was going to swindle me out of it. As far as I knew, he was a wealthy man." After a chop of silence, she added, "When I first got to Dallas, I rented the apartment I have now, and he would stay with me when he was in town. He took me out from time to time, but he never introduced me to any of his friends or family. He said that he couldn't, not while he and Megan were still keeping a lid on their divorce. I didn't know anyone in Texas besides him, so there was no one for him to meet, either."

"Sounds like your life with him was isolated."

"It was. But at the time, I didn't mind." She winced, hating the stomach-clenching ache that repeating this story gave her. "It seemed romantic, just the two of us. But then he started to seem troubled. Only he refused to tell me what was wrong. He kept saying that he didn't want to burden me with it. It was obviously part of his ploy, pretending to protect me from his problems. But finally, he told me that he was under financial duress. That his personal accounts had been frozen because of something Megan had done, and he wasn't able to make withdrawals or use his credit cards. He also said that he couldn't withdraw money from his business accounts, either, because he didn't want to involve his family, and they were tied to those accounts. He was trying to solve it without them knowing what was going on."

Rand shook his head. "It sounds like he had it all worked out, blaming his wife while trying to get money from his girlfriend."

"I loaned him little bits at a time, until the amounts started getting bigger and bigger. But even so, he never gave me cause to think that he couldn't be trusted. He promised that he would pay me back, and I believed him. The last time I saw him, he said that he was getting close to sorting it out and should have access to his accounts again." She took a long sip of soda to quench her suddenly dry throat, then went on. "Shortly after that, I received a letter from an attorney saying that he was dead, and I was named as one of the heirs to his estate."

When she hesitated, Rand motioned for her to continue. She took one more sip of her drink before she said, "I was devastated by his loss. Then later, of course, things took a different turn. I discovered that he wasn't even Will Sanders. I also learned that four other women had received the same letter, also making them heirs to an estate that didn't even belong to him. It made me feel as if he'd stolen from me twice, first by taking my money. Then by making me part of an inheritance I wasn't able to claim."

Rand nodded, a bit too solemnly. "Did you ever tell your family about him? Do they know he's the reason you had to borrow money from them?"

"I told them a condensed version of the truth. I admitted that I came to America to be with a man and that he'd taken advantage of me and hurt some other women, too. I couldn't reveal the entire story since we're not allowed to discuss the case with anyone who isn't involved in it, but they're still concerned about my emotional well-being. They could tell how badly this affected me."

"And now you're going to tell them that I helped you through it and you fell in love with me."

"Yes." She would be deceiving them about what should be the most important events of her life. Falling in love. Finding her true soul mate. Accepting his marriage proposal.

"It'll be okay," he said, much too softly.

Was he comforting her for the lie she was going to tell her family? Or was he consoling her for Rich's treachery?

Whatever he was doing, it made her feel warm and protected. When she was a girl, eating Ma's bread-and-butter pudding used to make her feel the same way. Sometimes she used to sit by the fireplace on cold nights and devour the entire pan.

"Do you have a preference for the type of engagement ring I get?" he asked. "The cut of the diamond? Or the kind of setting?"

She cleared her mind. She wasn't supposed to be feeling warm and protected by Rand. She hadn't even decided how trustworthy he was. "I thought you were going to get an antique one?"

"I am, but this will be the first time I'll be buying jewelry for someone other than my grandmother. And I want to do it right."

"I'm sure you'll do splendidly with whatever you choose. But I'll be returning it to you after the marriage ends, so you should get something that has a good resell value so you can get your investment back."

He frowned. "I don't want it back. It's going to be your ring. I'm buying it for you."

"I know, but it wouldn't be proper for me to keep it."

"Then you should be the one to sell it and recoup what you lost."

"That isn't necessary," she insisted. "Besides, I already told you earlier that I don't want to be beholden to you."

"Come on, Allison. You should at least get a diamond out of this deal."

She wasn't comfortable getting anything out of it except her green card. "Maybe we should discuss this another time. I don't want to argue on our very first day."

"All right, we'll figure it out later." He paused before he asked, "Do you know your ring size?"

She shook her head. She'd never worn a ring before, on any of her fingers. She didn't own much in the way of jewelry, aside from the costume stuff that she kept in a small wooden box, all tangled up together.

He said, "There must be a way to measure it. I'll look it up online." He checked his phone. "Oh, here we go. There's a paper method that should work. I'll print this and we can try it." He got up from his seat. "I'll be back in a minute."

While he was gone, she stayed at the dining table, reminding herself to breathe. Within no time, she would be Rand's wife. She would be sleeping upstairs in that scandalous boudoir, with her hot-as-sin husband on the other side.

He returned with the paper chart and a pair of scissors, striding back into the room and catching her eye.

As he stood next to her chair and cut out the ring sizer, she asked, "When are you going to announce our engagement?"

"You mean publicly? I'd rather wait to make a splash until after we're married. We've got too much to do, trying to plan the ceremony this quickly. If we get bombarded with media attention beforehand, we'll never get everything done."

As he took hold of her left hand to size her finger, his touch sent an electric current through her. She nearly jolted from the feeling. Thankfully he didn't seem to notice.

"You're a six." He set the chart aside. "I'm going to have to wear a ring, too. I need to look as husbandly as I can, to flash my status as much as possible. But I'll find myself a plain gold band. Not an antique. Just something simple and modern."

"Yes, plain bands seem to be what most men prefer." Or so she assumed. "Would you mind if I took an Uber back to Dallas tonight, instead of you taking me?" She needed some time alone, to sit quietly in her apartment and try to quell her anxiety. "But you can come over tomorrow, if you want."

"That's fine. I can stop by after I get your ring. We should probably go to the county clerk's office tomorrow, too, to apply for our marriage license. You'll need to have your birth certificate and passport handy for that."

"I will." She thought about his social media followers. "I hope your hordes of female admirers don't hate me for taking you off the market."

"There isn't a person in their right mind who could hate you, Allison. You're just too damn sweet." When she bit down on her bottom lip, he stared at her. She stared back at him, until he said, "Now give me your phone, and I'll give you mine so we can program our numbers into them."

Once that was done, she arranged for her car.

He waited outside with her, with the sun getting lower in the sky. He didn't kiss her goodbye; he didn't put his wickedly delicious mouth against hers. They didn't hug, either. They didn't do anything that rang of affection.

Then, right before she left, he reached out and smoothed a strand of her hair away from her face with the merest skim of his fingers. A barely there touch that gave her that warm, snug, bread-and-butter pudding feeling again.

Even long after she got home.

The following day Allison bustled around her apartment, sweeping the floors, vacuuming the area rug beneath the coffee table and fluffing the decorative pillows on the sofa. True to his word, Rand was on his way over to give her the engagement ring he'd purchased and then take her to the county clerk's office with him.

After she finished tidying up, she smoothed her simple cotton dress and combed her hair, checking her reflection in the bathroom mirror. She looked as ordinary as she always did, except maybe a tad more flushed.

About ten minutes later the doorbell rang. She answered the summons and greeted Rand. He was as dapper as ever, dressed in casual clothes, his broad-shouldered body filling up the tiny space on her stoop.

She invited him inside, and he glanced around and said, "This is a cute place, a nice little studio."

"Thank you." She'd tried to make it seem more like a one-bedroom by dividing the sleeping area from the living area, but she wasn't able to block her bed completely. A portion of it was still visible, on the other side of a bookcase.

Thankfully, he didn't mention it. But why would he say something about her bed?

"It's bright and sunny," he said.

Allison nodded. Was he getting the small talk over with before he presented her with the ring? "I like bright spaces." But so did he, she realized. He had lots of windows in his house. Most of her light was coming from a sliding glass door that led to her patio.

He asked, "Are you keeping this apartment for after the divorce or are you planning on getting a different one?"

"I was going to come back here." She couldn't afford to start over somewhere else. "Why? Do you think me keeping it is going to be a red flag with Immigration?"

He appeared to be contemplating a solution. "We can say that we're going to use it as our Dallas residence, for those times when I have meetings in this area. Since Spark Energy has an office not far from here, Immigration shouldn't take issue with that."

"Initially, I chose this apartment because Rich suggested that I acquire one near the office where he primarily worked." The same Dallas office Rand had just referred to. "And now this location is factoring into my arrangement with you."

"Everything is going to factor into our arrangement."

That was certainly true. She gestured to the kitchenette. "Would you like a beverage? I should have offered you something before now." She was normally a better hostess than this. But being in such tight quarters with this hot, sexy man was distracting her, especially with her bed being so doggone close. It just seemed so intimate somehow. "I've got iced tea in the fridge."

"No, thanks. I'm fine." He reached into his front jeans pocket and removed a small cloth pouch. "Here's your ring." He opened the pouch and dropped the ring into her hand, treating it like a free-falling gumdrop. "It's an Edwardian piece with a European-cut diamond. But it's not part of a set, like I thought it would be."

"Oh my stars." She gazed at the object glittering in her palm. "It's exquisite." The center stone was mounted in an ornate platinum setting with lacy scrolls and brilliant emerald accents.

"The dealer told me that in the Edwardian era, women usually wore their engagement rings on a different hand than their wedding rings because both rings were so intricate they didn't always match up too well. That's why this isn't part of a set. But I got a small platinum-and-diamond band that will complement it, so you can wear them together. I didn't bring that one with me. I figured I'd save it for the wedding day."

"Should I put this one on now?"

"Sure. Let's see if I sized you correctly."

She slipped it on her left hand. It fit perfectly. "It's exactly as it should be."

"I chose it because of the emeralds. I figured that a green-eyed girl marrying a green-eyed boy should have some emeralds."

"That's a lovely sentiment." But the bridelike feeling it gave her was making her head spin.

He tucked the empty pouch back into his pocket. "Promise me that you'll keep it after we split up. I don't want the first ring I gave someone to be meaningless. I really want you to have it."

Mercy, she thought. Now how was she supposed to refuse? To even the playing field, she said, "All right, but this will have to work both ways. I'll buy your wedding band instead of you getting it for yourself. And you'll have to keep it afterward, too."

He smiled, shrugged. "I don't have a problem with that."

She glanced at the dazzling diamond on her hand, wondering what she'd gotten herself into, making a pact with him to keep their rings.

"Did you talk to your family?" he asked. "Did you tell them about us?"

She redirected her focus. "Yes, I did." She gestured for him to sit, and they proceeded to the sofa. "I spoke to them first thing this morning. Ma cried, just as I knew she would, and offered to remake her dress for me. She said that she could tell how in love I was, just by the sound of my voice. But I did lay it on pretty thick." Allison was still suppressing the guilt that caused. "Now Da, he didn't react as well. He wanted to be sure that I wasn't jumping into anything too soon. Or that I wouldn't end up getting hurt again."

"Given the circumstances of your last relationship, I can understand his concern."

"I told him that you're a good man and you'd never hurt me." Something she hoped and prayed was true. With her track record, she wasn't the best judge of character. "I had to warn him about your reputation, though. I didn't want him Googling you and finding out on his own."

He made a tight face. "I hope you convinced him that I changed my ways."

"I certainly tried. But I think he'll feel better after you video chat with him."

Rand gentled his expression. "I'll do what I can to help put him at ease. By the way, I was thinking that you should probably pack up some things and start staying with me."

"You want me to move in this soon?"

"Why not? We need to get used to being around each other. It'll be easier to arrange the wedding if we're already living together, too."

He was right. It didn't make sense for her to keep going back and forth from Dallas to Royal. "I can move in tomorrow." Since she wasn't giving up her apartment altogether, all she had to do was pack her essentials. "Will that be soon enough?"

"That's fine."

"Is it all right if I bring my plants to your house? I have some fairy gardens on my patio, and I don't want to leave them behind. They'll die if I don't keep watering them."

"You can bring whatever you want," he reassured her. "I'll help you haul your things over. But truthfully, I don't even know what fairy gardens are."

"Come on, I'll show you." She took him through the sliding glass door and onto her patio, where her creations were. "See, each one is a miniature garden, with living plants, designed as a place for fairies to frolic." She'd used clay pots for the containers, some of them purposely broken or chipped, so the tiny structures inside of them were more visible. "I wrote an article a while back about how popular fairy gardening has become around the world, particularly in the States, and I got so fascinated with it, I decided to build my own once I came here."

He knelt to observe the work she'd done. She watched as he examined the glitter-speckled stones, the moss-covered cottages, the glass mushrooms and wooden bridges. He studied the wee-bit fairies themselves, too.

She said, "In Ireland, some of our fairies can be dark and sinister. But these fairies aren't like that. They have goodness in their hearts."

He was still looking at them, squinting at how small they were.

She continued her tale, "But just because they're kind, doesn't mean that they aren't without mischief.

If we're not careful, they might capture us on our wedding day and whisk us off to the Land of the Young." She turned dreamy, imagining how it would be. "It's an enchanting place, a supernatural realm of everlasting youth and beauty. But once we're there, we wouldn't be able to come back, at least not at the risk of turning old right away."

He stood to his full height. "Is that part of your folklore or did you just make that up?"

"It's real." She sent him a silly smile. "Are you sure you still want to marry me?"

He smiled, too, and laughed a little. "I'll take my chances." With a more serious tone, he added, "But for now, I think we should go to The Bellamy on our wedding night. I can book one of their honeymoon packages, so it'll seem as romantic as it's supposed to be. Come to think of it, I should Instagram some pictures of us while we're there. I think that'll be the most effective way to let the masses know we're married, straight from the honeymoon."

She hadn't considered where they would be spending their wedding night. But now that he'd brought it up, her traitorous body had gone much too warm, her blood surging through her veins in short silky bursts.

"We can do a newspaper announcement, too, with a traditional wedding photo," he told her. "But we can do that after our hotel stint. I'd rather reach out on social media first."

She had to ask, "What kinds of honeymoon pictures are you talking about?"

He pushed his typically tousled hair away from his

forehead. "Just some cozy shots that make us look like a blissfully happy new couple. 'Cause what the heck, right? That's got to be safer than being whisked away to a supernatural realm."

Allison nodded, even if she didn't agree. Getting cozy in a honeymoon suite with him didn't sound safe at all.

Four

Rand poured himself an orange juice from the wet bar in his bedroom. With the way he was feeling he was tempted to add vodka to it, but he refrained. It was too early for a cocktail, so he drank it the way it was.

His video chat with Allison's parents had just ended, and it had gone exceptionally well. But it was an uncomfortable reminder, too, of how important he was already becoming to her family.

He glanced at the double doors between their rooms. Allison was on the other side of them, putting her belongings away. He'd helped her bring her stuff over this morning, including the fairy gardens. They were in his backyard now, on the patio near some other potted plants, where Allison could see them from her window. She'd chosen the spot herself.

He left his empty glass on the bar, strode over to the doors and rapped on one of them, giving it a musical rat-a-tat-tat.

She called out, "Come in!" No hesitation whatsoever, but she was expecting a full report from him on how the chat went with her folks.

He opened both doors, leaving them wide-open, and entered her suite. This was the first time anyone had ever occupied it who wasn't going to straddle his lap or purr like a kitten in his ear, and it gave him a strange sensation to see her there. With her casually ponytailed hair and makeup-free complexion, she looked as cute and fresh and off-limits as she was.

He glanced at the bed, where she stood, and where some of her clothes were piled. The rest of them were already hanging in the walk-in closet, which was nearly the same size as her entire apartment. He'd built the closet for his fashionista lovers. Allison certainly didn't need one that big. Her wardrobe was modest, at best.

He moved toward her, without getting too close to the bed. She would be climbing under those very covers tonight. Whether she slept buttoned up, scantily clothed or full-on naked, he couldn't say. But thinking about it sent a carnal shiver through his blood.

"How'd it go?" she eagerly asked.

He cleared the heat from his mind and got straight to the heart of it, the stuff that had been hard for him to swallow. "You were right about how much your dad adores you. He made me promise to protect you with my life."

She made a pained face. "Da can be over the top sometimes."

"It made me feel like a medieval swordsman or something, vowing to safeguard his maiden. I've never been in a position like that before. But I handled it okay." By making a commitment he wasn't going to keep, by pretending to be far more honorable than he could ever be. "He gave me his blessing to marry you."

"Well, thank goodness for that." She sat on the edge of the bed, near her clothes.

"I could tell that he liked me. I liked him, too." Angus Cartwright was a good-natured man, a hardworking sheep farmer, with thinning gray hair, a booming smile and wire-rimmed glasses. By comparison, Rand's father had been the head of a financial institution—a tall, trim, tight-ass CEO who rarely smiled. "Your grandfather jumped in to meet me, but I barely understood a word he was saying. His accent is really thick, and I think he was tossing in some Gaelic words to trip me up."

She laughed. "Granda has a wicked sense of humor."

He managed a laugh, too. "So I gathered." He went serious again. "You were right about your family wanting us to get remarried in Ireland. Your dad mentioned that to me."

She sighed. "How did you respond?"

"I told him that maybe we could do it next year

sometime. I was just trying to buy us some time, and then he suggested our first-year anniversary. So I went ahead and agreed to that."

"You did the best you could under the circumstances."

He'd certainly tried. "When your dad introduced me to your mom, she kept staring at me, marveling at how handsome she thought I was. She went a little nutty over my eyes and how similar the color is to yours. She said that we were going to have the most beautiful green-eyed babies ever born."

"How embarrassing." Allison covered her face with her hands, peering at him through her fingers. When she lowered them, she said, "But I told you she was meddlesome."

"Yes, you did." Sheila Cartwright was as sweetly intrusive as a parent could be. "I didn't mind that she thought I was handsome, but the kid thing kind of freaked me out. I didn't know what to say, so I told her that I gave you a ring with emeralds because of how alike our eyes are. She started crying after that and praised me for being handsome *and* romantic."

"At least you made a good impression on her."

He nodded. At this stage of the lie, they had to fool their families before fooling anyone else. "Your mom told me that I'm not allowed to see you in your dress before the ceremony. She also said she was sending you a little silver horseshoe to put in your bouquet for some extra-special luck. She explained that in the old Celtic way, women carried around real horseshoes on their wedding days, but now they do it with small symbols of them."

"Ma has always been superstitious, in all sorts of ways."

"That's what I figured. But she's also one of the kindest people I've ever met. She treated me as nicely as anyone ever has, and it's obvious how much she loves you." Sheila's maternal nature made Rand miss his own mother and a pang of longing went through him. "You're lucky to have her in your life."

Allison smiled with pride. "Thank you."

He studied her from where he stood. "You resemble her." Their glossy red hair, their fair skin. "It makes sense that she would want you to wear her dress." And now that he was prohibited from seeing his bride before the ceremony, he was even more interested in how she was going to look.

"Did you happen to meet my granny? Or my brother?"

"Your grandmother was waving in the background when your mom was talking to me. Your brother wasn't there. I guess he was in London. But I let your mom know they could all attend the ceremony on Skype, and that made her cry all over again."

"You've had quite a morning, with Ma bawling at you."

"You warned me ahead of time that she was going to cry." He thought about how quickly the divorce was going to roll around. "What are you going to tell your parents when we split up? How are you going to explain it?"

"I'll probably just say neither of us was as ready for marriage as we thought we were. That Da was right when he was first worried about us rushing into it."

"We can use that story with everyone. But people will probably think I'm the one who screwed up. You're too sweet to get blamed."

"No one should be blaming anyone, not if we part as friends. I'll tell everyone that you tried to be the best husband you could be."

"I appreciate that." But the promises he'd made to her dad were still weighing on him. "Your family is going to be disappointed in me when it ends."

"They'll be disappointed in me, too. They won't understand why I'm giving up on my marriage so easily. But I'm never going to tell them the truth."

He pressed his lips into a grim line. "I've still got a lot more lies to tell. I'm going to head over to my brother's place to talk to him today."

"Is he expecting you?"

"Yes." And Rand just wanted to get it over with. "I didn't tell him why I needed to see him, but I said it was important. I haven't told my grandmother yet, but I'll do that later today, too. But as befuddled as her short-term memory is, I'm not going to wear her down with an in-person visit. I'm just going to call her." He exhaled roughly. "She'll probably forget bits and pieces of what I tell her, and I'll have to repeat it before the wedding, anyway. And with how rushed everything is, I might not get the chance to introduce you to her until that day. But we can spend some quality time with her after we're married."

She walked over to the other side of the room, settling on a spot near a window, where the sun illuminated her. "How do you think she's going to feel about you getting married in such a rush? Or getting married at all?"

"She'll be fine with it." He took a moment to observe Allison, to appreciate how natural she looked in the light. She wasn't what most people would consider beautiful, but now that he was getting to know her, he thought she was getting prettier and prettier. Was it any wonder he was eager to see her in her wedding dress? "Nothing I do bothers my grandmother."

She tilted her head. "Your reputation never bothered her?"

"No. She always encouraged me to do whatever felt right. To be impulsive if that suited me. To live life in whatever manner made me happy." And for now, he wished that he could be the playboy he'd always been and seduce the hell out of Allison before their marriage ended. But he didn't have the right to prey on her innocence. Rich had already done enough damage in that regard, and Rand didn't want to fall into the same category as that conniving bastard.

"Your grandmother must be an open-minded woman."

"For not trying to rein me in? She shook things up in her day, too. She had her one and only child, my mother, out of wedlock. Things like that were scandalous back then, especially in her high-society world. But it was her choice to be a single parent. She didn't even tell the father about the baby."

Allison's eyes widened. "Really? How come?"

"He wasn't someone she was going to stay with, so she didn't think it was necessary for him to know. She never talked about him to anyone, either. She kept his identity hidden." Rand cleared his throat. "She met him on a trip to Europe, so no one from her inner circle saw them together. But in his country, he was really famous. Everyone knew who he was there."

Allison's all-too-curious gaze locked on to his, right before she asked, "Do you know who he is?"

"Yes." Rand's grandfather was one of the most notorious Spanish matadors who'd ever lived. "She told me when I was heading off to college. She told Trey when he was an adult, too. But we promised her that we would keep it between us."

"I understand respecting your grandmother's privacy." She frowned, tiny lines forming between her eyebrows. "But I hope he didn't take advantage of her. I hope that isn't the reason she didn't stay with him or tell him about the baby."

He sensed that Allison was thinking about Rich and all of the women he'd used. "It wasn't like that. He wasn't a bad person. But he wasn't the settle-down type, either."

"What happened to him? Is he still around?"

"No. He died a long time ago, so it's water under the bridge, anyway." Nonetheless, Rand felt a kinship toward his grandfather because his grandmother had told him how similar their personalities were. They even looked remarkably alike. He changed the subject, moving on to a more pressing issue. "I should head out to see my brother before he wonders what's taking me so long. I wish it wasn't going to be so difficult, though."

She moved away from the window. "Do you want me to go with you?"

"Thanks, but I need to do this alone." To face whatever Trey threw at him, without subjecting Allison to it.

"Is this a joke?" Trey asked with an incredulous expression.

"No, no joke." Rand had driven straight to his brother's bachelor's pad in Houston to deliver the marriage news. But as expected, his younger sibling refused to accept it.

Trey leaned against the kitchen counter, attired in his running clothes, his face unshaven, his brown eyes narrowed. As a youth, he'd been a star athlete, excelling at every sport he played. He could've gone pro, but he'd decided to enlist in the United States military instead, intent on saving the world.

Typically, Rand and his brother got along well. They'd always been close, often banding together when their dad bullied them. But their dad's influence had made them scrappy at times, too, and if they didn't see eye-to-eye on something, it could get tense between them. Like now, Rand thought.

"Come on." Trey goaded him. "What's really going on?"

"I just told you, I'm in love and I'm getting married."

"To who?" His brother all but scoffed. "Some spoiled rich party girl?"

Rand held his ground, as tightly as he could. "I'm marrying Allison Cartwright."

"The Irish woman who was at Will's funeral? Are you serious?" Trey grabbed his water and took a swig. War hero that he was, he had a sharp mind and a cautious nature, keenly aware of the people and places around him.

In this case, his suspicions were justified, but Rand wasn't letting up. "I got close to her after the funeral. She was in a bad way, and I helped her through it."

Trey wiped the back of his hand across his mouth. "Since when have you ever helped anyone?"

"You make me sound like a prick." Rand was already feeling like one, after all the romantic jargon he'd heaped on Allison's family today. "I donate time and money to charitable causes all the time."

"That's not the same as being there for a woman who needs you. All you ever do is jump from one lover to the next, and now you're marrying someone who isn't even your type."

He clenched his jaw. "You don't know anything about Allison."

"I know that she sat there at Will's funeral looking like a broken bird. She seemed devastated by everything that went down."

"And I just told you that I helped her through it," Rand said. "That she needs me. That I need her. That we've been having a secret relationship."

"I wouldn't put it past you to sleep with her, but to fall in love, to marry her? I just can't believe it."

"Well, you better start believing it because we're in the process of planning our wedding." Rand battled a tightness in his gut. His brother was wrong about him sleeping with Allison. But he couldn't say anything about that. "Just accept that I've changed. That she changed me. That we're in love and eager to have a life together."

"I wish I could, but something just doesn't feel right about this. Are you sure you're telling me the whole story? That you're not up to no good?"

Well, shit. Rand tried another tactic. "Do you remember when we were kids and I used to dress up as Batman, and you would trail along as Robin? Well, this is sort of like that, only so much bigger, so much more important. So just stick by me, okay? I came here to ask you to be my best man." At least he wasn't lying about that. "I need your support."

"Oh, wow." Trey staggered a little. "You really are serious about getting married."

"I absolutely am." If he failed to pull this off, if he didn't repair his reputation, he would probably fail to bring in the new client at work and lose his job, too. But damn it, Rand had paid his dues at Spark Energy Solutions. He'd worked his way up the corporate ranks, becoming Will's right-hand man, and now he needed to prove to the board of directors that he was every bit the CEO that Will believed he could be. That Rand wanted to be. That his critical father would never have given him credit for. "We're going to get married as soon as we can, right after the Fourth of July."

"Then of course I'll support you. I'll be your best man. But I still have my concerns. Even if your heart is in the right place now, how long will it be before you panic and want to go back to being single?"

Rand hated this conversation, despised it, in fact. It wasn't easy having his brother see through him. Robin was supposed to be Batman's sidekick, not his analyst. "That's a terrible thing to say to a groom."

"I'm sorry. I was thinking about Allison. She seems like a nice person, and I just don't want to see her get hurt."

Rand's gut went tight again. He was getting the same warning from Trey that he'd gotten from Allison's dad. "I'm not going to do anything that will hurt my wife."

"So you're going to love, honor and protect her, the way a husband is supposed to do, for the rest of your life? That's a hell of a commitment for anyone to make, but for a guy like you, it's major."

"I know, but I'm going to do it." Rand pushed the boundaries of his lie for the second time that day, making lifelong promises he knew deep down he wasn't capable of keeping.

Allison awakened with a cluttered mind. She hadn't slept well. She'd spent most of the night thinking about Rand and how he was on the other side of those big fancy doors. Somewhere in the wee hours, she'd even fantasized about entering his suite, via those doors, and slipping into bed with him. Even now, she wondered what it would be like to explore the depth of her sexuality and have a head-spinning, smoking-hot affair with the man she was going to marry. But as fun and naughty as that sounded, becoming his lover would be even more complicated than becoming his wife. Because the sex would be real, even if the marriage wasn't.

Allison would do well to keep her knickers on. She'd already gotten herself into a painful mess over her affair with Rich, and she needed to learn from her mistakes and comply with the no-sex clause that *she herself* had come up with. She just wished that she wasn't so physically attracted to Rand. That was a complication she could do without.

Preparing to face the day, she entered the bathroom, soaking in the big, glorious tub her suite provided.

A short while later, she donned a carefully considered outfit—a neatly ironed blouse and capri pants—and headed downstairs.

She found Rand in the kitchen, brewing coffee, and as quick as that, she nearly swallowed her tongue. Was this how it was going to be every morning? The man wasn't even properly dressed. The hem of his shirt hung loose, the buttons completely undone. His chest and stomach were casually exposed with impressive pecs, a nifty navel and irresistible abs. Intensifying his appeal was that messy midnight hair, still damp from the shower.

She honestly didn't know where to look. Every part

of him was making her warm and foolishly aroused, reigniting her forbidden fantasies. Her nipples were even peaking beneath her bra, rubbing abrasively against the fabric. But thankfully, they weren't showing through her top. She actually glanced down at her chest to be sure.

After that, she settled her gaze onto the floor and noticed that Rand's feet were bare.

"I made enough coffee for two," he said.

"Thank you, but I drink tea." Difficult as it was, she spoke as normally as she could. "I sometimes drink up to six cups a day."

"That's good to know. We're supposed to be learning each other's habits. But for now, I don't have any tea."

"I brought some with me." She darted past him and opened a cabinet to the left of him. "I put it in here."

"Really, when did you do that?"

"When you were at your brother's yesterday."

He grimaced. "What an ordeal that was. But at least he's lending his support, even if he thinks I'm going to be a crappy husband."

Allison didn't reply. Just thinking of Rand as her husband, crappy or otherwise, was enough to make her knees weak. Standing beside him now, she prepared her morning beverage while he poured his.

He said, "I've got ham-and-cheese frittatas in the freezer, with roasted red potatoes and sautéed mushrooms on the side. There's fresh-cut tropical fruit ready to go, too. Will that do for our first breakfast together?"

"That sounds yummy. I guess it's safe to assume all of that came from the chef delivery service you use?"

Rand nodded. "It's convenient, especially for a bachelor like me."

"I can cook for us while we're married."

"Are you sure you wouldn't mind doing that?"

"I'm positive. I like to cook as much as I like to eat. But for the record, I like to keep active, too." She wanted him to know that she was more than just a foodie. "I grew up playing rugby. I was in a league, right up until I came to Texas."

"Really? Well, you're just full of surprises." He went to the freezer and opened it. "I played college ball. I was a linebacker."

He certainly appeared to have the size for it, with that big strong body of his. When he rummaged through the freezer, she ogled his butt. He turned back around, and she glanced away, even though she wanted to run her greedy gaze along his abs.

While he placed their meals in the microwave, she sipped her tea as nonchalantly as she could. He drank his coffee, as well.

The buzzer dinged, catching his attention. After he transferred their food onto plates, he put the fruit in a large glass serving bowl.

They dined at a long marble island, which served as a kitchen table, leather-and-wood barstools already in place. She wished that he would button his shirt while they ate. But he didn't. She was still subjected to his half nakedness.

"We'll have to challenge each other to a match sometime," he said.

"A match?"

"Rugby. Football."

Oh, right. The sports they played. "Yes, we can do that." As long as he kept his shirt on, she thought. Otherwise, how was she supposed to get into a game without drooling all over him?

They both kept eating, until he said, "So what sort of stuff do you normally cook?"

"All sorts. But I can make some traditional Irish meals you can reference during our immigration interview, if they ask you any questions that pertain to my culinary skills."

"It's impossible to know what they're going to ask. But if they ask you about mine, you can always tell them that I don't cook." He rose to refill his half-empty coffee. "I've never had a traditional Irish meal. I like to vacation abroad, though. I have a private jet at my disposal, with a pilot standing by when I need him. But I've never been to Ireland."

"Why not?" She would've pegged him for someone who'd traveled just about everywhere.

He resumed his seat with the steaming beverage in hand. "Because I've never dated anyone from your country and typically I only go where the women are."

She shook her head, letting him know how odd his statement sounded. "The last time I checked there were women in Ireland."

He shrugged, smiled. "You know what I mean."

Yes, she understood. He was referring to his international string of lovers. "So I'm going to be your first Irish woman?"

"That's certainly how it's going to seem. But technically, you aren't really mine."

If she gave into temptation and slept with him, would she become his? Definitely not, she told herself. He didn't commit to his lovers. Besides, she shouldn't even be thinking about things like that. "None of your women belong to you, at least not for very long."

"Yeah, me and my lothario ways. I'm a bad boy cliché in this town." He leaned back in his seat. "So, what's your favorite color? If I had to guess, I'd say it was pink. I noticed a lot of pink clothes in your closet yesterday."

"I definitely like pink. But for the sake of us being together, I would choose green." For the color of their eyes, for the emeralds he'd given her. She lifted her ring to specify, making her reason clear. Then she asked, "What about you?"

"I've never had a favorite color, so if that's a question in our interview, you can say I don't have very many favorite things. I do have a favorite word." He waggled his eyebrows. "But it's a dirty one."

Instead of being coy, she brazenly asked, "Is it the F-word? Because if it is, I've never heard you say it."

"Yes, that's it." He slipped into a mock whisper. "But mostly I only say it when I'm...*you know...*"

When he was what, doing the act itself? Or telling his lovers that was what he wanted to do to them?

She tried to brush it off, even if she'd gotten dizzily aroused. Now she wanted to hear him say it, for his spicy Texas twang to slide straight into her. "That isn't something we'll be discussing during the interview."

"No, I don't suppose it is. But can you imagine if it was, if the immigration officer asked us a bunch of questions about our sex life?"

"I'd rather not picture a scenario like that." And especially not after she'd awakened this morning consumed with wild urges about him.

"Yeah, I guess not. But they might ask if we use contraceptives and what type we use. I heard they sometimes ask things like that."

To unmask couples, like them, who aren't sleeping together? "What should we say if that comes up?"

"I use condoms. But if you're on the Pill or something, then we should probably say that since it'll coincide with your medical records."

"I'm not on anything. Condoms would be my choice, too." She thought of a related topic. "What about children? What if they want to know if we plan on having kids?"

He angled his head. "Do you want them?"

"Yes, someday. Two would be nice. Maybe three."

"Then that'll be our story. Two, maybe three little ones. And with green eyes, no doubt, like your mother said."

Envisioning having bright-eyed babies with him was getting her flustered. She took a second helping of fruit and nearly spilled it onto the table, before it reached her plate.

"So what's yours?" he asked.

"My what?" His question confused her.

"Oh, sorry. Favorite word. Or don't wordsmiths have favorites?"

"We do. Or I do, anyway." She struggled to relax, to get the sex and baby subjects off her mind. "It changes, depending on what I'm writing. When I was plotting my book to be a historical, I was rather fond of rake."

He chuckled. "Like the gardening tool?"

She rolled her eyes, but she laughed a little, too. She was glad he'd made a joke. It helped lessen the tension. "I was talking about the other kind, the one that's used to describe a hell-raising man. Rake is short for rakehell."

"I didn't know that's where it was derived from. But raising hell can sure be fun." He winked mischievously. "Of course I can't do that anymore."

"You definitely need to behave yourself." Husbands shouldn't be rakes, and fake wives shouldn't be lusting after them. "We have a marriage to concentrate on."

"Speaking of which…since Trey is going to be my best man, you should have a maid of honor, too."

Allison sighed. If she was in Kenmare, she would have a slew of childhood friends and chatty cousins vying for that spot. But here in Texas, she was just getting to know people. "Maybe I can ask Megan since she's the woman I feel closest to in this town. I first met her at the funeral, and we started to bond after that. A strange bond, I suppose, over being betrayed by the same man, but it's been nice having her as a new friend."

"I think she's a great choice. Let's keep the guest list to a minimum to make things simpler."

She nodded. "Should the guests be allowed to bring a plus-one?"

"Sure. If they want to. But no more than that." He set his fork down and swallowed the last of his coffee. "I'm going to head upstairs to finish getting dressed." He stood and carried his plate over to the sink. "I have to go into the office today. I have a few meetings, but I'll try to be back early."

"That's fine. I should go upstairs, too, and call Megan. My cell phone is in my room." Since she was also done eating, she got up and loaded her plate and flatware into the dishwasher, along with his. She didn't like leaving dishes in the sink.

He thanked her, and as they went upstairs together, he said, "We should use this for the wedding."

"Use what?"

"This." He gestured to their current whereabouts. "The stairwell. You could come down it in your dress, and I could wait for you at the bottom. I've seen weddings like that on TV, where they incorporate the stairs as part of the bridal walk."

"That's lovely. I like that idea." She was impressed that he'd thought of it. "But if we do that, the rest of the ceremony should take place inside the house, too."

"That makes sense. But I'd rather have the reception in the backyard. Is that okay with you?"

"Yes. An outdoor reception sounds nice. We're

going to need a color scheme. How about the colors that are in my ring?"

"That works for me. We can figure out the rest of the details and order the flowers and decorations and whatnot after I get home today. We'll have to decide on a menu and what type of food to serve, too. I have a great caterer we can use."

She furrowed her brow. "Will they be able to accommodate us so quickly?"

"I hope so. If not, we'll have to find someone else."

Suddenly Allison was getting overwhelmed with everything they had to do to prepare for the wedding. "When I was a young girl dreaming of getting married, I never imagined it happening like this."

"Just think of how I feel," he said, as they turned simultaneously in the direction of their rooms. "And how I never planned on getting married at all."

Five

While Rand was at the office, Allison tried to make good use of her time. She ran some errands, then met with Megan for a late lunch. They dined together at the Royal Diner, an informal eatery with a decidedly retro vibe. The red vinyl booths and checkerboard floors reminded Allison of the old American malt shops depicted in movies. In keeping with the atmosphere, she ordered a cheeseburger, French fries and a chocolate shake. Megan chose a soup-and-salad combo.

They sat in a corner booth with no one else around. Overall, the diner was quiet. The lunch crowd was gone, and it was too early for the dinner folks.

Gazing across the table at her friend, Allison couldn't help being enthralled with Megan. She was just about the most beautiful woman Allison had ever seen, a glamorous brunette with long wavy brown hair and big blue eyes. Megan was a socialite who owned a designer shoe company, a strong, intelligent, highly capable woman, so different from the way Rich had described her.

If Allison could be honest, she would gladly tell Megan that she was marrying Rand for her green card. Megan, of all people, would understand that after the way Rich had brought Allison to the States and humiliated her, she needed to restore her self-worth and remain in Texas on her own. But this girl-talk meeting wasn't about the truth; it was about pretending that her marriage to Rand was the real deal.

"Thank you for agreeing to be my maid of honor," Allison said. "It means a lot to me."

Megan smiled. "I wouldn't miss it for the world."

"I'm sorry for not giving you much notice."

"Don't worry about the timeline. I can handle it." Megan skewed a forkful of lettuce. "However, to be perfectly honest, I am rather stunned that you and Rand got together. I never would've envisioned you two as a couple. But I think it's wonderful, too."

"We knew that we were going to shock people. But we're very much in love." Playing her part, Allison made a dreamy expression. She was supposed to be a blissful bride, after all. And sometime in the future she would be, just not with Rand.

Gorgeous, tempting, sinfully sexy Rand, she

thought wistfully. If only her forbidden fantasies about him would go away.

"What colors are you using for the wedding?" Megan asked.

Trying to clear him from her mind, Allison hastily replied, "I decided on green and silver, or platinum, to be specific, to complement my ring." The diamond flashed as she turned her hand. The emeralds glittered, too.

"It's a gorgeous piece, absolutely dazzling on you." Megan admired the Edwardian setting with what appeared to be a well-trained eye. No doubt she had plenty of fine jewelry of her own.

"Thank you." Allison was still getting used to the luxurious weight of it, mindful not to snag the ring on her clothes or leave telltale threads wrapped around the prongs. "You can wear any style of dress you want in either or both of the colors."

"Should it be formal or something in between?"

"Semiformal will do. I'm wearing a traditional gown, but it's not a designer dress or anything like that. It's the same one my ma married my da in. We decided on a small, private ceremony at Rand's house, but you're welcome to bring a guest." Allison drank more of her milk shake. "With how we're hurrying to get everything done, we're trying to figure things out as quickly as we can."

"It sounds beautiful. I'm pleased to be part of it." Megan abandoned her salad and crumbled crackers into her soup without taking a bite. "Weddings should be joyous occasions."

Suddenly Allison wondered what Megan's wedding to Rich had been like. When she'd married him, she'd believed that he was Will, and now the real Will was back. Allison couldn't fathom how Megan was handling that. Megan's brother, Jason Phillips, was a childhood friend of Will's. Presumably, Megan had grown up around Will, too. Was it awkward between them now? Or had they become closer, bound by the impostor case? Did Megan have feelings for Will? And how did he feel about her?

Whatever was happening between them, Allison decided not to ask. Prying into her friend's personal business while lying about her own just didn't seem right. For now, Allison needed to get a grip on her own emotions and figure out how to make her short-lived marriage to Rand work.

On the night before the wedding, Rand couldn't sleep. He had a million thoughts running through his mind and most of them concerned Allison.

He glanced at the double doors that separated their rooms. He assumed his bride-to-be was still awake. A bright amber light glowed beneath the doors. He took a chance and knocked.

A click sounded, and she opened one side.

She immediately asked, "Rand? What's going on?"

"I just wanted to have a last-minute talk."

"Come in." She stepped away from the open door.

Rand entered her room, the suite he'd built for his lovers. But of course Allison didn't resemble anyone he'd ever shared a bed with before. She was attired in a modest pajama top and matching bottoms, a strong indication that she wore clothes to bed. Rand sure as fire slept naked. His lovers did, too, particularly when they crawled under the covers with him.

"How are you holding up?" he asked, pushing past his wayward thoughts.

"I've got the jitters." She held out her hands to show him how unsteady they were.

In addition to her shakiness, he noticed the sparkling white polish on her fingernails. He glanced down. Her toenails glittered, as well. He assumed it was her mani/pedi in preparation for tomorrow.

"I'm nervous, too," he said. But he was trying to keep his anxiety inside, where it didn't show. "I keep hoping that we didn't forget anything." Planning a wedding this quickly was like entering a cake-and-flowers war zone. They'd even worked through the Fourth of July holiday, missing local picnics and fireworks displays. But they would be attending a Stars and Stripes fund-raiser after the honeymoon, giving them time for a patriotic gathering later. "You seemed emotional this morning when your dress arrived, but I didn't say anything about it." He wasn't even sure if he should be mentioning it now.

"When I opened the box and saw Ma's gown, it made me sad to think I'll be wearing it for a marriage that isn't going to last." She twisted her ring, turning it halfway on her finger. "But that's my fault. I should have come up with an excuse to not wear it."

"I'm looking forward to seeing you in it."

She quit toying with the diamond. "You are?"

He nodded. "I like that it's special to your family. That it has a unique history. I also like that you and I are becoming friends." To him, there was no other way to describe the anxious bond they'd begun to share—the whirlwind that had become their wedding.

In the next bout of silence, the acknowledgment of their friendship turned a little awkward. But that didn't stop him roaming his gaze over her, from thinking how tempting she looked in her plain and simple pajamas. It made him want to touch her, to hold her, to pull her close to him. But most of all, he wanted to kiss her.

"You know what might help us relax?" he asked.

She blinked. "No, what?"

"We should kiss. Shift," he clarified, using the phrase she'd taught him. He needed an excuse to taste her, all the way to his harried-groom soul.

Her voice quavered when she said, "We've only kissed that one time, on that very first day."

"That's why I think we should do it now." On the eve of their wedding, he thought, looking into the familiar greenness of each other's eyes. "Only we should do it longer and deeper than before." He moved forward. "Do you want to try it and see if it helps?"

"Yes." She agreed with anticipation in her voice.

He reached for her, taking her in his arms. "How's this for starters?"

"It's nice, so very nice." She went breathy. "I like how close you are to me."

He trailed his hands down her spine. "And I like how curvy you are. Like one of those old-fashioned pinups." Even in her proper pajamas, her body was lush and full.

"No one has ever compared me to a calendar girl."

"You have the figure for it." He inched lower, cupping her rear and giving her a good, stiff jolt with his zipper.

"Now you're just being a rake." She smiled, laughing a little.

A rake. A rakehell. A hell-raiser. With those words spinning in his mind, he took her mouth, hard and fast, making her gasp. He felt her sharp intake of breath. But he'd warned her how long and deep this was going to be.

He sparred with her tongue, creating a shock of heat and wetness. She clung to him, digging her nails into the back of his shirt. He manhandled her ass, gripping it tighter, keeping her roughly bound.

When they came up for air, it was only for a second, just enough time to dive under again, openmouthed and carnal.

He rubbed against her, and she reacted with a moan. He liked how easily affected she was, how everything he did triggered a response. Her honey sweetness exploded inside him, and he kissed her over and over, making the most of her reactions, of his all-consuming need.

If they were lovers, he would be yanking off her pajamas by now. But she wasn't his lover, and he needed to end this before he got carried away. He pulled his mouth from hers, and they stared mindlessly at each other.

She stumbled a few steps back. Neither of them spoke, until she bit down on her bottom lip and said, "I hope this isn't going to sound strange, but I took an interest in you when I was still dating Rich, when I thought he was Will."

He stumbled now, too. "How did that come about? You hadn't even met me until the funeral."

"I know, but since he never introduced me to anyone, I Googled some of his friends and coworkers to see who they were. And you fascinated me like no other," she confessed. "You fit the bill for my book hero, so I started checking out your Instagram pictures and reading gossip tidbits about you online. I developed a bit of a crush on you, but I didn't tell Rich about it. I get crushes on actors and singers, too, so I didn't think it mattered."

It sure as hell mattered now, Rand thought. Her sweet little crush gave him a big hard thrill. But he downplayed his reaction. "I don't mind you modeling your book hero after me, except for the part where your heroine tames him." He'd already told her that would never work on a guy like him, but he decided it bore repeating.

"My book is going to be fiction," she reminded him. "Like our wedding."

He nodded. "I should probably go now." His hunger for her had already reached its limits. If he didn't leave, all hell might break loose.

"Yes, you should leave." She fidgeted with her ring again. "We both need to get some sleep."

"I'll see you tomorrow." The ceremony was scheduled for early in the day, accommodating the time difference across the sea. "Dream well, Allison."

"You, too, Rand."

With a quick nod, he walked away. Just as he crossed the threshold into his own room, he glanced back and saw that she was watching him, like the uneasy bride she was about to become.

This was it, Rand thought. He and Allison were getting married. He stood at the bottom of the stairs garbed in a black tuxedo, a white rose boutonniere pinned to his lapel.

To keep from hyperventilating, he took a deep breath, preparing to become a husband and show the rest of the world how much he'd supposedly changed. A husband who couldn't make love with his wife, he thought. Even with as much as he wanted Allison, he was honor bound to keep his hands to himself.

Rand couldn't see the guests, as his back was to them. All of them, including Allison's family on Skype, had a view of the staircase. Grandma Lottie brought her caregiver to keep her company, and Trey brought a date. Megan had chosen to come alone. But nonetheless, Rand had asked everyone to surrender their phones upon entering the wedding. He didn't want anyone taking pictures or videos and posting them publicly before he was ready to announce it on his social media pages. Instead, he'd hired a photographer who was already snapping away, getting images that Rand could use as he saw fit. A professional videographer was filming the festivities, too.

Once the music started, Rand's heart thudded in his chest. He'd hired a harpist to play the Celtic song Allison had chosen for the wedding music. The same harpist would be entertaining them at the outdoor reception, immediately following the ceremony.

But for now, he was fixated on his bride. She glided down the stairs in a delicate, white-lace gown. The collar was high and ruffled and the sleeves were long and sheer. She looked as fresh and lovely as a country maiden, a crown of wildflowers adorning her red hair. She wore it pinned up, with loose tendrils framing her face. He suspected that her mother was crying about now, seeing how beautiful her daughter looked.

Rand smiled at Allison, hoping to ease both of their nerves. She returned his smile and finished her descent. He took her arm and they made the turn, both of them now facing their guests. With the Celtic song still playing, they approached the justice of the peace, who waited in front of a floor-to-ceiling window, sunlight spilling in from the yard.

After the music stopped and Rand and Allison were in position, Allison handed Megan her white-rose bouquet. Nestled within the flowers was the horseshoe ornament that had been included for luck.

The vows were simple and quick to recite. Trey was in charge of the rings, and he had them readily available. Rand placed the diamond-studded band on Allison's finger that complemented the engagement ring he'd given her. She slipped a thick gold band on him, and he noticed that it wasn't as plain as he'd assumed it would be. A leafy design was engraved on it. He didn't understand the symbolism. He would ask her later when they had time alone to talk.

Soon they were prompted to kiss. After the way they'd kissed last night, slanting his mouth over hers felt as warm and natural as he'd hoped it would be. She reacted with a girlish sigh, as if their feelings for each other were real.

The kiss ended, and they faced their guests. Allison waved to her family on Skype. Her mother was definitely crying. So was her grandmother. Rand noticed that Grandma Lottie had tears in her eyes, too, and she barely knew Allison. They'd met briefly this morning, while Allison was getting ready for the ceremony. But Lottie seemed impressed with Rand's bride, nonetheless. She'd already told Rand how "sweet" Allison was.

A knot formed in the center of his chest, knowing how downhearted all of these loving, caring people were going to be when he and Allison got divorced. Even Trey would be disappointed, and he wasn't expecting the marriage to last.

But Rand and Allison were putting on a damned fine show.

At the reception, they smiled happily and accepted well-wishes and toasts.

During the meal, Rand took the liberty of kissing his wife in between bites. She returned his kisses, then fed him tasty morsels from her plate. He liked this part of being married. Cutting the cake was fun, too, as was licking the icing off each other's fingers.

No one could deny how hot and hungry the bride and groom were for each other.

Later, while they moved on the makeshift dance floor, swaying the way couples in love were supposed to, Rand said, "Thank you for the engraving on my ring. That was a nice surprise. But what is it and what does it mean?"

Allison nuzzled closer to him. "It's a branch from a heather plant. Since we incorporated some Irish themes into the wedding, I thought a Celtic engraving on your ring would jazz it up. Heather stands for dreams, romance and attraction." She pressed her lips to his ear. "I know none of this is real, but it's going to make my dream of staying in the States come true. And with the book-hero crush I have on you, the romance and attraction part seemed fitting, too."

Her explanation deepened his desire for her, making him wish that he could consummate their marriage tonight. But they weren't even going to be sharing a bed. He would be sleeping on the sofa in their honeymoon suite.

He whispered to her. "Have I told you how wholesome I think you look in your dress? So soft and pure."

"You make me sound like a virgin." She spoke in a hushed tone, too, keeping their conversation private. "I suppose it is a virginal dress. But the designer nightgown Megan gave me isn't. It's sleek and sexy. Of course, there's no way I'll be slipping that on."

"She gave you a sexy nightgown?" Damn, now that

was all he was going to think about. "Will you at least bring it to the hotel and show it to me?"

She nodded. "I'll toss it in my suitcase and let you see it."

"Can I touch it, too? Maybe press it against myself or something?" He glanced down, making her aware of the part of himself he was referring to.

"Rand." She gasped. "I can't believe you just said that."

Neither could he, but if getting off on her nightgown was the extent of his pleasure, he just might do it. "What color is it?"

"It's a bright shade of emerald. She got it to match the wedding colors."

"Remind me to thank her later." Rand spun Allison around on the dance floor and kissed her one more time, long and slow, with forbidden thoughts encased in his mind. Even if nothing was going to happen, he could at least pretend that he was going to make love with his wife tonight.

Six

The Bellamy was inspired by George Vanderbilt's iconic French Renaissance chateau, and the luxurious decor in Allison and Rand's suite reflected that theme, but on a newer, trendier scale. The custommade furniture, constructed from deep rich woods, shimmered with metallic accents and contemporary engravings. All of the latest gadgets and high-speed technology was provided, as well.

This was definitely a modern honeymoon, Allison thought. Soon after they arrived, they started taking pictures for Rand's social media pages. He orchestrated the selfies, and she followed his lead. He suggested they wear hotel-monogrammed robes with their swimsuits underneath. Hers was a classic onepiece. She had too much breast and hip and butt for those little stringy things. But thankfully she was covered in the photos, her robe securely fastened. Being in her bathing suit in front of Rand was difficult enough. She didn't want strangers seeing her, too.

At the moment, she sat next to him on the sofa in the living room area, going through the images.

"This is a great shot," he said, holding his phone closer to her. "It's my favorite."

She leaned over to check it out. "It is nice." They definitely looked like romantic honeymooners, bundled in their thick white robes, with a bottle of Dom Pérignon between them.

He tapped on another picture, opening it to its full frame. "I like this one, too." A close-up he'd taken of their hands, their rings beautifully showcased.

She agreed it was effective. "How many are you going to post?"

"Just these two. That should be enough to get the ball rolling. I'll keep the hashtags simple. I'll write something uplifting, too, about how incredibly special my new bride is and how she turned me into a one-woman man."

"I'll post something tomorrow." Allison's social media pages were private. Only close friends and family would be able to see whatever she chose to put out there. "But you can post whatever you want tonight."

"I'll take care of it right now. Why don't you relax in the hot tub and I'll join you when I'm done?"

"Okay." The hot tub was located on a private deck attached to their room. Their accommodations were exceptional, but Rand obviously had his choice of suites. He knew the billionaire owners of the hotel. His world was so different from Allison's.

She grabbed a couple of towels, proceeded to the deck, fired up the jets, removed her robe and sank into the water.

She closed her eyes and lost track of time, unsure of how many minutes had passed or how much longer it would be before Rand came outside.

Allison just hoped the internet trolls didn't pick her apart. She feared that Rand's followers wouldn't think she was glamorous enough for him. While she understood that he thought of her as innocent and was promoting her as his hopelessly romantic, Irish-country-girl wife, she wished she was comparable to his other women. Just once, she wanted to turn heads.

"I brought the Dom."

She opened her eyes. There stood Rand holding a tray that contained two long-stemmed flutes and the champagne chilling in a silver ice bucket.

He placed the tray beside the hot tub and said, "I figured we should partake in this instead of just using it as a prop."

She nodded and asked, "How did the posts go?"

"They're already starting to get reactions, especially the picture of the two of us. In any event, we'll probably be trending in the top posts by morning. It should get picked up by the gossip blogs following me, too." He sat on the deck. "Ready for some bubbly?"

"Yes. Absolutely." She'd only had a few sips of

champagne at the wedding. Besides, she wanted to relax and stop worrying about how Rand's followers were going to react to her.

He popped the cork with a heart-thumping bang, filled both flutes and handed her one.

She tasted it and moaned. He smiled and ditched his robe, exposing his godlike body, his swim trunks as stylish as everything else he wore. He settled into the water, right next to her, and she nearly squeezed her thighs together. He was so close she could smell the lingering cologne on his moonlit skin.

"I should have brought you a snack," he said. "I put the chocolate-covered strawberries the hotel sent up in the fridge, but I can go get them."

"I'm fine." The only thing she was hungry for was her wild-spirited husband. But he wasn't on the menu.

"Oh, wow." He teased her. "You're turning down food?"

"Not just food, but chocolate."

"You must be losing your mind."

She most definitely was, with how badly she wanted him. But sleeping with him wasn't a prudent thing to do. She'd known it when she'd first agreed to marry him, and she knew it now, as rationally as before.

Using the champagne as her consolation prize, she drained her flute and grabbed the bottle for a refill.

About fifteen minutes later, she was on her fourth glass and appreciating the giddy sensation.

"You better slow down," Rand warned.

"I'm just a tad tipsy." Enough to act like an eejit and crawl onto his lap.

He looped his arms around her waist. "I shouldn't be letting you do this."

She ignored his concern and kissed him, snaring his tongue, giving him the kind of shift good girls shouldn't give.

Was she grinding his crotch? Was she making him hard? Yes, indeed, and it felt damned good. Water swirled around them, the jets shooting extra heat in their direction.

So much heat, so much lust. He got harder and harder, devouring her mouth and treating her like his guilty pleasure. But it didn't last.

After a slew of scrumptious kisses, he pulled back. "We need to stop."

"And I think we should keep going." She grinded against him some more and thought about the expletive he favored. "You can whisper your favorite word in my ear, all hot and dirty, before you do it to me."

He groaned in agony and nuzzled the damp ends of her hair. "I'm not doing anything to you that you're going to regret later."

In what was left of the rational side of her brain, she knew he was right to refuse her advances. She was in no condition to make sound decisions. But with the fantasies she'd been having about him, she could hardly blame herself for her behavior. Of course that just might be the champagne talking.

She said, "Fizzy alcohol makes a person drunk faster. I read a scientific study about it."

Rand kept his hands wrapped around her waist. Whether he was trying to stop her from moving around on his lap or savoring the bump-and-grind before he let her go, she couldn't be sure.

"I heard that, too," he replied. "But there's an old saying that the bubbles go straight to your head."

"I think it has more to do with the stomach than the head. But my brain does feel fuzzy." Allison kissed him one last daring time and felt him shudder, his aroused state making her smile.

She climbed off his lap and settled back down in her seat. When she reached for the champagne, he snatched the bottle away from her.

"Oh, no you don't." He poured it out, right onto the deck, where it pooled. She thought it looked like a puddle of pee.

She giggled at her goofy little metaphor. "That's a waste."

"The only thing wasted is you. Come on, sweet girl, let me get you up and ready for bed."

"I'm not even slurring my speech." Even if she was light-headed, she wasn't sloshing her words. Soon she might be. But for now, she was holding her sentences together.

"I'll give you credit for that." He eased her out of the water, and they stood on the deck.

She frowned; she swayed on her feet. Steadying herself, she reached out and traced a tingling hand down his abs, following the muscular ripple.

"It's not fair that you're so hot," she said.

"Yeah, I know. I'm your hottie book hero. Now

let's get you dry." He cloaked her with a towel, using it to pat her down.

He was still wet. She watched watery rivulets run down his gorgeous body and drip into the spilled champagne. He was standing in the puddle. So was she.

After he finished drying her, he hastily toweled himself off. Next, he helped her into her robe, the way an old-fashioned suitor might aid a lady with her coat. He even knotted the belt for her. He left his robe on the deck and she was secretly glad he was still bare. She didn't want him to cover up.

They entered the suite, and he led her to the bedroom. "Where are your pajamas?"

"Still in my suitcase. I'll go get them." She dug through her luggage, flinging items to and fro. He shadowed her like a watchdog.

She found the nightgown Megan had given her and tossed it to him. "This is for you."

"Cripes." He caught the long, silky, see-through garment. "This isn't a good time for sexy lingerie."

She glanced up and grinned. Rand clutched the fabric as if it might scorch him. She imagined it setting his big, hard body on fire. "It's okay if you press it against yourself like you said you were going to do."

A muscle jerked in his jaw. "Just get your PJs, Allison."

"Maybe I'll wear that." She tried to tug the nightgown away from him, but he held tight, banning her from having it.

"Spoilsport." She searched for the conservative pajamas she'd brought, plucking them from the pile of clothes she'd dumped on the floor. "I hardly ever drink, but I have to admit I'm enjoying myself." She motioned to the lingerie in his hands. "And don't forget, you're free to enjoy that."

The nightgown fluttered from his fingertips as he dropped it back into her suitcase. "I'm going to strangle you when you're sober."

She shrugged, and he guided her toward the bathroom.

"I'll wait here for you," he said, letting her know he would remain outside the door.

Before he nudged her inside, she glanced back and sent him a starry-eyed look. "You're a protective husband."

"I ought to be, with all the pledges I made."

She smiled and closed the door. She liked how protective he was. It made her feel warm and melty inside. She removed her robe, fighting the knot Rand had tied, and peeled off her swimsuit. She didn't feel steady enough to shower, so she climbed into her pajamas just the way she was and left her bathing suit and robe balled up together on the floor. However, she managed to brush her teeth. She never went to bed without proper oral hygiene.

She returned to Rand and said, "I forgot to get my underwear out of my suitcase. I don't have anything on under these." She flapped her baggy pin-striped bottoms. "Normally I wear knickers. Sometimes I even wear a sleeping bra. I don't want my breasts dangling to my knees by the time I'm an old lady."

He dropped his gaze. "They look plenty perky to me."

"They're too big." She straightened her spine, jutting out her chest, letting him take his fill. "I always hated being busty." But not tonight, she didn't. Tonight, she appreciated what God had given her. And much to her drunk-and-flirty satisfaction, her nipples had come out to play, creating noticeable peaks under her top.

He continued to stare.

She went delightfully smug. "My eyes are up here, mister." She pointed for effect.

He lifted his gaze, his voice going warm and soft. "I know where those green eyes of yours are."

Now she really felt as if she were floating. He sounded beautifully romantic. When he tucked her into bed, she decided that he was the best husband a bride could have. He kissed her forehead and turned out the light, leaving her alone, steeped in bubbly dreams on their wedding night.

In the morning, Rand cursed himself for being a gentleman, especially when Allison stumbled out to the breakfast table. He could have made love with his wife last night. He could have done wild, wicked things to her. Yeah, he told himself. He could have taken advantage of her while she was drunk, and that would have made him the worst kind of jerk.

She was no longer in her pajamas. She'd changed

into a plain T-shirt and lightweight sweatpants. He could tell that she was wearing a bra, her breasts curvaceously bound. He assumed she had panties on, too. But her cautious attire only heightened his desire for her.

"I took a chance and ordered for you," he said. "Eggs, pancakes, the works, in case you're the type who eats her way out of a hangover." With her appetite, he assumed she might be. He gestured to the aspirin he'd left on her napkin. "That's for you, too."

"The food looks fab. I do have a bit of a headache, but I'm not feeling as bad as I thought I would be. I think breakfast will help." With a sheepish smile, she ducked her head. "I feel stupid about the way I acted last night. I'm embarrassed about it now. I should have known better than to drink like that."

"It was fun seeing you so uninhibited." Of course the raging hard-on she'd given him hadn't been particularly fun, not when he'd restricted himself from doing anything about it.

"You're not going to strangle me now that I'm sober?"

He winced. "You remember me saying that?"

"I remember everything."

So did Rand. Every pelvis-grinding rub, every tongue-tangling kiss, every loopy, sexy thing she'd said to him. The nightgown Megan had given her was burned into his brain, too.

Allison swallowed the aspirin with her juice and placed the napkin on her lap, settling in to eat. "How did you know when to order?"

"I heard the bath running." He'd showered earlier when she was still crashed out. He'd stood under the spray and let the water pummel him.

She glanced at the individual-size teapot in front of her. "Thank you for taking such good care of me."

"No problem." He watched her fix her tea, pouring milk into her cup before she added the steeping brew.

"How are the Instagram posts doing? Is the photo of us trending today like you thought it would be?"

"Yep." He drank his coffee while she sipped her tea. "The gossip blogs grabbed hold of it, too. They featured it with headings like 'Instafamous American playboy takes proper Irish bride.' One site is calling us AliRan."

She smothered her pancakes in syrup. "Oh, my goodness. They gave us a celebrity-couple nickname?"

"It was paired with a question asking people how long they thought it was going to take for you to realize you'd made a mistake and run for the hills. Get it? AliRan. They even made a meme of it. But I expected stuff like that to happen." He'd been in the public eye long enough to know how the media worked. "I shared the meme on my page with a caption that says AliRan represents you running toward me, not away from me."

"That was a good way to twist it in our favor." She seemed impressed with his marketing savvy. "What types of comments are people making?"

"Overall, my followers are being kind and congratulatory. I blocked a few of them who posted snide things. Unfortunately, I can't do anything about the comments on the gossip sites."

She made a troubled face. "What are they saying?"

"Some people think that you're going to get your heart broken by a womanizer like me. That a seemingly nice girl like you deserves better. And others think I should have married someone who was—"

"Prettier? More glamorous?" she asked.

"Yes, but that's a bunch of bull. You're perfect the way you are." With her dazzling green eyes and shiny red hair, killer body and quirky sense of humor, she was absolutely radiant. "I like everything about you. Besides, no one knows the real us."

She frowned at her tea. "The real us is a lie."

He went after his eggs, eating a forkful before he replied, "We're still real people with real feelings."

"If the public knew that I married you for my green card, they wouldn't think I was so nice. And if they knew about my affair with Rich, they'd probably think I was a bitch for sleeping with a married man."

"As far as you knew, he was getting divorced. And after what that bastard did to you and everyone else, you'd still come off as nice." He didn't have an answer about the green card situation. They would both be crucified for that. But no one was going to find out. They would protect that lie to their dying days.

She heaved a heavy sigh. "Were there any positive comments on the gossip sites? Or did everyone trash us?"

"Lots of people jumped in to defend us, saying that we make a fascinating couple. They're anxious to see our wedding photos. I'm going to post one later today, so it'll start circulating. The photographer emailed the images to me this morning. We can go through them after breakfast."

"Are you still going to do a formal announcement in the newspaper?"

"Definitely." He intended to make a splash in the Royal and Dallas society pages. "We have to strike while the iron is hot. Our honeymoon picture is only going to be trending for a day or so. I'm not the kind of 'celebrity' who stays at the top." He wasn't an entertainer or reality star or athlete. And hadn't acquired a following for being an entrepreneur or visionary or business trendsetter, either. He'd gotten noticed for being a Texas millionaire who took flashy selfies and played around. "AliRan isn't going to become a household name."

She flashed a grin. "You mean we're not going to turn into Kimye or Brangelina?"

"Nope." He laughed a little. "But we can milk AliRan for what's it worth and show everyone what a loyal husband I am while it still matters." His first step to becoming a respected CEO was to clean up his image, and by God he was trying.

"When are we going to fill out the green card marriage application?" she asked.

"If you're up for it, we could do it online today."

"Sure. The sooner the better." She dipped her eggs into the leftover pancake syrup pooling on her plate and took a bite. Damn, he thought. Last night she was kissing and rubbing and making him hard, and this morning he was getting turned on by watching her eat. She glanced up, and they stared at each other, caught in a sexually charged moment. Their marriage was a business arrangement, where temptation wasn't supposed to apply, so he'd better get ahold of himself.

And fast.

Rand had no idea what he was going to do after the divorce or how soon he would start dating other women again. But for now, he wished that he didn't crave his wife as badly as he did.

His only comfort was that she appeared to be trapped in the same dilemma, wanting him as much as he wanted her.

After Allison and Rand came home from The Bellamy, they were inundated with cards, boxes of candy and gift baskets, mostly from Rand's coworkers and business associates, congratulating them on their nuptials.

Although Allison helped him sort through them, her mind was elsewhere. She was nervous about an upcoming fund-raiser at the Texas Cattleman's Club, especially since the club catered to such an elite crowd. Rand was a well-known TCC member, and this would be her first public appearance with him. She didn't want people at the fund-raiser to judge her the way she'd been judged online. She wanted to look pretty, as glamorous as any other woman there.

Maybe she should call Megan and talk to her about it. She could ask her friend to help her shop for a dress and to get ready that night. It was certainly worth a try and better than fretting about it on her own.

Rand checked the card on an elegantly arranged fruit-and-gourmet-cheese basket and said, "Oh, wow. This is from Brisbane Enterprises."

She didn't know who that was, but she took an educated guess. "Is that the company the board of directors wants you to bring in as a new client?"

He nodded. "The CEO's name is Ted Marks. He's the guy who hasn't been returning my calls." He waved the card. "And now he's saying that he and his wife will be attending the Stars and Stripes fundraiser at the club and are hoping to see us there."

The black-tie event she was so nervous about. "That sounds like a good sign."

"Definitely. I used to run across them at other functions in the past, and they never gave me more than a passing nod. Of course it hadn't mattered to me then. I'll bet his wife is curious about you. From what I heard, she has a strong influence over him."

The thought of Ted Marks's wife taking a curious interest in Allison only intensified her pressure. "What are Ted and his wife like?"

"They're both older, midfifties, proper, the conservative-society types."

She studied the fruit basket. "I'll do my best to make a good impression on them." Which meant looking and feeling her best that night. She was definitely going to call Megan for help. "What's the wife's name?"

He rechecked the card. "Sharon."

"Ted and Sharon Marks. I'll look them up online so I'll recognize them when I see them."

"That's a good idea. There are probably pictures of them together at other fund-raisers." He sent her an appreciative smile. "Thanks for offering to do what you can to make a good impression."

"It's the least I can do." She understood how important the Brisbane account was to him. It factored significantly into why he'd married her. "But I could really use a bit of unwinding now."

"With what?" His smile morphed into a wicked grin. "A bottle of champagne?"

"Ha-ha. Very funny." She was never going to live that down. Nor would she ever forget the desperate heat of straddling his lap. "I was thinking more along the lines of our one-on-one football-rugby match."

"You want to play right now? Sure. Let's do it. But with me being so much bigger and stronger than you, I think I should give you a lead."

"No way. We're playing fair and square. I don't want you going easy on me." She stood tough. "No gender bias."

He roamed his gaze over her. "You'll probably knock me out with those boobs."

She rolled her eyes. Along with her champagne fiasco, she was never going to live down her complaint about her breasts being too big. "You better be prepared to get your arse kicked."

"By a girl?" He looked her over again, teasingly, brutishly. "You're dreaming, sweetheart."

"Did you seriously just call me sweetheart?" Now

he'd gone and done it. "For your information, I played in one of the most successful leagues in Ireland."

"One of the most successful *women's* leagues. Look at me, Allison." He made a badass gesture to himself. "There's no way you're going to beat me."

"Oh, really? Well, how about this? If you win, I'll be your maid tonight. I'll do whatever chores you require. And the same applies if I win. I'll get to use you as my houseboy."

"Your houseboy?" He laughed, ridiculing her suggestion. "As in me doing domestic chores for you? Good luck with that."

His chauvinistic confidence was going to be his downfall, of that she was certain. "Shake on it?"

"Hell, yes." He gripped her outstretched hand. "But we're going to have to use an American football. I don't have a rugby ball."

"That's fine." She took her hand back. "There's not enough of a difference to matter. You can set the rules, too."

"Are you sure you don't want me to give you a lead?"

"I'm positive." She wasn't taking charity for a sport she'd triumphed in since childhood. "We both need to change. Then we can meet in the backyard."

"It's your funeral. But don't say that I didn't warn you."

"Likewise." She tore off up the stairs before him.

In no time, he shot up behind her with his heavy male footsteps pounding the wood. He was already breathing down her neck, behaving as if he wanted to tackle her right then and there. Allison only smiled, eager for the match to begin. She wanted nothing more than to knock her big, strong, arrogant husband down to size.

Seven

Whoop! Whoop!

Allison did the happy dance. She jumped and gyrated and wiggled her hips. She clapped and rejoiced in her victory. She'd won the match!

It hadn't been easy; she would probably have bruises on her bottom, given how many times she'd hit the ground. She'd never played a more challenging game. But she'd scored more points than Rand. She'd managed to tackle him, too, to knock him tail over teakettle.

In fact, he sat on the grass at this very instant, glaring up at her as she danced.

"Don't be such a sore loser," she said, still whirling about.

He grabbed her ankle, sending her off-kilter. She

stumbled and fell, landing next to him with a thud. He laughed and rolled on top of her, pinning her beneath his linebacker's body.

"Who's in charge now?" he asked.

"This doesn't count. I already won." But by goodness, he was heavy. She couldn't get away if she tried.

He stared down at her. "You won because I let you."

"That's hogwash." She was certain that he'd played his best game. "I'm faster than you, and you know it." She'd outrun him when it mattered. "You underestimated me, and it cost you the game."

"All right, so you took me by surprise. But now I've got you, and you can't escape."

"You're still going to be my houseboy." She frowned. "Unless I gave you a concussion. You have a cut on your forehead." She gently touched the area around the wound. "It's bleeding."

"That's no big deal. I'm totally clearheaded. I'm even aware of how damn sexy you look right now."

"You're flirting with me, after I just kicked your arse? Now I know you're concussed." She tried not to swoon. Being called sexy by him was making her heart pound. She skimmed his hair away from his eyes. "Let's go inside and I'll clean that cut and put a bandage on it."

"Okay. But I'm only agreeing because I like it when you touch me." He lifted his body from hers, like a panther releasing its prey.

Allison stood and dusted herself off. "I've got first-aid supplies in my bathroom." She gestured for him to follow her.

They went upstairs together, and Rand sat on the closed lid of the commode while Allison dampened a washcloth at the sink.

She wiped away the blood on his forehead. "The cut's not as deep as I thought it was."

"I knew it wasn't anything to be concerned about." He watched as she doctored him. "But it feels nice to be cared for."

After dabbing an antiseptic ointment on the cut, she fumbled with the paper wrapping on the bandage.

"I don't think I need that," he said.

"And I say you do." She fitted the flexible material to his skin. "You're all set now."

His gaze locked on to hers. "I like it here."

Did he mean *here* in her bathroom with her standing between his legs? If that was his implication, she liked it, too. His primal scent mingled with hers. They were both sticky with sweat and had grass stains on their clothes, too.

"You're supposed to be fulfilling your duty as my houseboy," she reminded him.

"So give me a chore, and I'll do it."

A crazy, wonderful, dangerously erotic task came to mind. Full-on lovemaking, she thought.

Allison couldn't deny how desperately she wanted her husband. He was all she thought about, dreamed about, fantasized about. But if she went through with it, she would have to be prepared for the consequences. But not all consequences resulted in adverse effects. Feel-good rewards were possible, too.

So was she going to do it? Was she going to give up the fight and have an affair with her husband?

Yes, by God, she was. If she didn't, she would never quit lusting after him. Yet it wasn't just the thrill of sex that drove her. Little by little, she'd begun to trust Rand and stop comparing him to Rich. Rand hadn't done anything to hurt her. He'd been kind and honorable all along. Just thinking about how gently he'd tucked her into bed on their wedding night made her want him even more. He could've taken advantage of her inebriated state, but he'd protected her instead. And now, on this post-honeymoon day, she craved every gorgeous part of him. But she wasn't going to regret her actions later. No remorse, she told herself, no self-condemnation.

Only heat. Only pleasure.

Instead of telling him what she had in mind, she said, "You can draw my bath."

"That's my chore?" His voice turned sandpapery. He even cleared his throat. "I wasn't expecting it to be something so personal. But if that's what you want, I'll do it."

She wanted a whole lot more. But for now, she was taking it slow. "You can pour some of my body gel into the water, too. To make it foamy." She walked over to a freestanding caddy. "It's this one." She lifted the blue-and-white bottle from the top shelf.

He approached the claw-foot tub. "How warm do you like the water?"

"However warm you think it should be." She stepped back, giving him carte blanche.

He turned on the faucet and let the water run. He tested the temperature a few times, adjusting it to a level that seemed to satisfy him. Then he asked, "Do you want to check to make sure?"

"I trust you." But trusting herself was another story. She was breaking all of her own rules.

He took the body gel from her, removed the cap and sniffed the contents. "It's nice. It smells like coconut."

"It's a Polynesian blend." Or that was how the product was advertised.

"How much of it should I add?"

"As much as you think it needs."

"You're making this hard on me."

He had no idea how *hard* she intended for things to get. But soon he would. "You lost the game. This isn't supposed to be easy."

He poured a capful of the gel into the water. When it didn't foam to his liking, he added more. "How's that?"

"It's perfect. I couldn't have done it better myself."

After the tub was full, he turned off the faucet. "There you go. Your bath is ready." He made a gentlemanly bow, exaggerating his duty to her. "I'll leave you alone now." He turned to leave. "I need to get cleaned up, too."

"You're not going anywhere."

He spun around, stopping in midstride. "What?"

She removed a fresh washcloth from a nearby

towel rack and tossed it into the water. "You're going to scrub my back."

He shook his head, backing himself against the sink. "That's not a good idea."

"It's part of your chore."

"Oh, yeah? Well, the minute you take off your clothes and climb into that tub, I'm going to want to do a lot more than scrub your back."

She shot him her best naughty-girl smile. She wasn't skilled at seduction, but she was giving it a heart-hammering try. "So who's stopping you?"

The ruggedness in his voice returned. "You're giving me permission to take what I want?"

"Yes." She most definitely was. But before she lost her nerve, she lifted her top over her head and tossed it aside. She removed her shoes and sweatpants, too. All that was left was her undergarments: plain white knickers and a shock-absorbing sports bra. Not exactly the type of lingerie designed for foreplay. But they'd served her well during the match.

Rand watched every move she made, his gaze darting from her ponytailed head to the wedding-white polish on her toenails.

He said, "This is pretty damned amazing, because after the hot tub incident on our honeymoon night, I've been having water fantasies about you."

"At least I'm sober this time." She was in control of her faculties. Or she was supposed to be, anyway. Her pulse roared in her ears.

He gestured for her to finish. "Go on."

Allison shed her bra, releasing her breasts. Her

nipples peaked the second they hit the air. Her knickers came next. She peeled them all the way down,
with her husband as her audience.

She sank into the bath. Surrounded by suds, she
swished the water and said, "It's your turn."

He didn't waste a coconut-infused second. He got
undressed and joined her, facing her, with his legs
parted and his knees slightly bent. The tub was big
enough for both of them, and she suspected that some
of his other lovers had invited him to share it with
them, too. She doubted this was new to him. But no
one else could claim to be his wife. That was her title,
at least for now, and it felt wonderful.

Beautiful.

Erotic.

Exciting.

Rand leaned forward and kissed her, his mouth
hot and thrilling against hers. She wrapped her arms
around him, dissolving into his fervid touch.

Once they separated, he bathed her. He ran the
cloth over her naked body, washing her everywhere,
spending extra time on her breasts and between her
thighs. Her eyes drifted closed. She was so enraptured
she could've been floating out to sea.

"Stand up, Allison."

She started and opened her eyes. "What? Why?"

"Why do you think?"

He smiled suggestively, deliberately, and his intention became clear. Oral sex: his mouth between her
legs. She'd never allowed anyone to do that to her.
She always thought it was too intimate, too private,

too embarrassing. But she wasn't going to refuse him. This was her awakening, her chance to be free. Being repressed wasn't part of the plan.

Still, she hesitated, taking a moment to grasp her newfound abandonment.

"Do you need help?" he asked. "Is the tub too slippery?"

"No. I've got it." As nervous as she was, she was excited, too. She proceeded to stand, offering herself to the man she married.

Rand gazed up at Allison, puzzling over her complexity. She seemed timid, yet anxious to be dominated. Or maybe in her own shyly sexual way, she was dominating him. This was her seduction, after all, her idea to bathe together.

"This is a first for me," she said.

He moved closer. "A first what?"

"You know." She gestured to him, down on his knees in front of her.

Holy hot-blooded hell. His pulse nearly jumped out of his skin. "No other man has ever…?"

"I've never been comfortable letting anyone touch me that way. And now here I am standing completely naked in a brightly lit bathroom, in an old-fashioned tub, with my husband…"

He liked that she narrated the scene, even if he was smack-dab in the middle of it. The verbal picture she painted was wildly arousing. So was the sudsy water snaking down her stomach and heading for the V between her thighs.

He wiped it away in one fell swoop. Then, eager to take what he wanted, he spread her with his fingers and tasted her with his tongue. She shivered on contact, and he repeated the sweet, slick process.

He glanced up to see if her eyes were closed. But they were wide-open. Little Miss Innocent was watching.

He licked and swirled, and she reached for his shoulders, using him as an anchor. He planted his hands on her butt, one on each cheek, prompting her to widen her stance.

She moaned, and he went no-holds-barred. He enjoyed turning on his lovers. But being the first to give Allison this kind of pleasure was exhilarating. She pitched forward, tugging her hands through his hair.

Everything she did, every reaction, encouraged him to take her to the next level, to ramp up the heat, pushing her further and further. He created sensations that he could see in her eyes. She was still watching him.

Rand pulled her closer, treating her to more of the same, and she came in a series of sticky-wet convulsions, pulsating against his mouth.

Upon her completion, she swayed on her feet. Sinking back into the tub, she smiled dizzily at him. Neither of them spoke. There wasn't anything to say. Allison looked as if she might melt and swirl, right along with the leftover foam in the water.

Rand wasn't done with her yet, but with her as loopy as she was, he gave her time to recover.

He continued their bath. He even released her ponytail and washed her hair, using a handheld shower attachment.

She sighed. "Everything you've been doing to me feels so good."

He nuzzled her nape. Presently, she was nestled between his thighs, her back to his front. "If I'd known how seductive losing a football match could be, I would have hurried up and lost it sooner."

She sighed again. "I haven't even done anything to you yet."

"You let me be the first guy to put his mouth on you. That's a major deal." It made him feel more important than any of her other lovers.

She leaned against him. "Do you want to finish this now?"

"Here, in the tub? I'd rather take you to bed." As tempting as her invitation was, he would prefer to roll around in the sheets, where there was more room to play.

"That sounds good to me, too."

"Then let's go."

They exited the bath, and once they were warm and dry, Rand carried his wife straight to her canopy-draped bed.

The crush Allison had on Rand before was nothing compared to how she felt now. This was turning out to be the most compelling day of her life.

While she waited to be ravished by him, he went to his suite to get protection.

He returned with a box of condoms, removed one

and put the rest of them in the nightstand drawer. "These are for future use. I still have extras in my room, too."

"You're such a responsible playboy." The Band-Aid on his forehead made him seem boyish. But his big, strong body was all muscle. "You deserve a merit badge."

He settled into bed with her. "You can give me one."

She reached between his legs. "Maybe this should be your reward instead." As she stroked him, the intensity of touching him rippled through her: the hardness, the silkiness, the power that radiated from him.

He smiled, and she glanced down. He was leaking at the tip. She circled him with her thumb, and he kissed her.

With lust shimmering between them, they closed their eyes and kissed some more, steeped in romantic rapture.

He lifted his mouth from hers, and she opened her eyes. His were open, too, and focused on her.

He roamed his hands along both sides of her body, following her shape, her curves. "Now I have to decide how to take you."

A hungry shiver slid down her spine. She assumed he was talking about sexual positions. "You can do it however you want." She just wanted him inside her, thrusting hard and deep. After what he'd done to her in the tub, she was more than ready for him.

He grabbed her, full-force, and they tumbled over the bed, messing up the covers. "I want it every way imaginable. I think I'm getting consumed with you. But no one has been forbidden to me before."

"I'm not forbidden to you anymore." She arched her hips, savoring the feeling. By now, he was braced above her, his chest upright, his pelvis pinned to hers.

"I know, but it still seems as if you are." He took the condom from the nightstand and tore into the wrapper. "There's just something about us being together…"

She bit down on her bottom lip. "Maybe it's the no-sex clause we're breaking."

"Yeah, that's probably it. This taboo thing we've got going on, with you seeming so innocent to me." He sheathed himself. "I've been trying all of this time not to corrupt you, and now here you are, being bad with me."

Allison keened out a moan. There was no time to formulate a reply. Not with how quickly he slid between her thighs and pushed inside.

He set a potent rhythm, and soon they were rocking back and forth, moving together, hot and slick and desperate. He caught his breath, and she wondered if his heart was machine gunning his chest. Hers thumped like mad.

He whispered something distinctively dirty in her ear, using his favorite word. She repeated it to him, and a sound akin to a growl rumbled from his throat. His feral behavior thrilled her, but she was being animalistic, too. She dug her nails into his back, probably leaving half-moon marks on his skin.

From his growl of approval, he obviously liked

it. So she clawed him with even more force, making the sex rougher.

A few breathless beats later, he rolled over, putting her on top. She straddled his lap, impaling herself and taking him all the way inside. He circled her waist, lifting her up and down. She leaned forward to kiss him, to devour his deliciously sinful mouth.

Nothing was ever going to be the same, Allison thought. Not after having Rand Gibson as her lover. She wanted to eat him alive.

Within no time, he maneuvered their positions again, reclaiming his place on top. Admiring his godlike presence, she thought about that very first day at the statue of Diana and how far they'd progressed since then.

He used his fingers to enhance her pleasure, driving her toward a release. Thrashing beneath him, her vision blurred and her brain went fuzzy.

She came in a flurry, making orgasmic sounds, lost in the forbidden sensation. She'd never been noisy in bed, but Rand made everything feel so wild and new.

While she morphed into a pool of mush, he spiraled toward his own core-shocking release. When it happened, he tossed back his head, the cords in his neck straining.

In the aftermath, or the afterglow or whatever it was supposed to be, his arms buckled, his body assailing hers with a masculine jounce.

She buried her face in his neck. "I think I just got tackled."

He laughed, his breathing labored. "Am I crushing you?"

"No." She enjoyed holding him this way, his nakedness warm against hers. She skimmed a hand down his spine, following each and every vertebra. "You can stay a while."

He didn't stay as long as she would've liked. He made his way to the bathroom to dispose of the condom. He returned and got back into bed with her. But he didn't lie down. He propped a pillow and sat up. Alison followed his lead and braced herself with a pillow, too.

He said, "If we smoked, this is where we would break out a pack of cigarettes and light up."

"Have you ever smoked?" There was still so much they didn't know about each other, so much left to learn.

"I tried it when I was a kid, but I didn't like it, so I never did it again. I assume you never have." He reached over to smooth her hair. "You don't seem like the type."

"Your assumption is correct." She appreciated the way he touched her, the gentle dusting of his fingers in her hair. He'd already done a splendid job of shampooing it.

He lowered his hand. "You're not going to go all wifely now that we did this, are you?"

She furrowed her brow. "Are you asking if sex is going to make me feel more attached to you?"

He nodded. "This could never turn real, Allison.

No matter how good it is between us, I don't have it in me to be anything more than a fake husband."

Something inside her went tight. Her chest? Her lungs? Her pride? All of the above? Shielding herself from the discomfort it caused, she said, "I can handle having an affair with you. Otherwise, I wouldn't have done it."

"I'm sorry. I shouldn't have doubted you. I guess I just got a sudden fear of how starry-eyed you are."

"I might be a hopeless romantic, but the last thing I want is to fall in love with the wrong man." She wouldn't—*couldn't*—lose her heart to Rand. "Being around you is helping me learn to trust again. But I'm not going to turn it into something more than friendship. Or desire," she added, letting him know how important the sex was. "It's just my cure for lusting after you."

He smiled and invaded her space, lifting her off her pillow and into his arms. "I don't know how I'm ever going to get enough of you."

"We're just going to have to learn to pace ourselves." She trailed a finger down the center of his chest, heading toward his abs and making his stomach muscles jump. "Maybe after this, we should wait a day or so to do it again."

"Are you suggesting that we deprive ourselves of what we want most?"

"Why not?" She liked the idea of rebuilding the tension, of putting each other under a torturous spell. "It'll make the next time even more exciting."

"Maybe so, but I'm not even done this time."

She pondered over him, this man who inspired her to play flirtatious games. "I'm not sure if that makes you incorrigible or insatiable."

"I'm both, especially now that I'm with you. But sex has always been my outlet."

"I think it's becoming mine now, too." She trailed lower. He was getting hard again. "And it's all because of you."

He watched her, his gaze following the movement of her hand. "So I really am corrupting you."

She gave him credit where it was due. "It feels amazing to be this free, this wild, and especially with you." Plus it was a whole lot safer than getting attached to him, she thought.

"Then I'm glad I could be of service." With a tongue-tangling kiss, he stole her breath.

A moment later, he went after another condom and nudged her legs apart, getting both of them ready for another hot, steamy, wickedly depraved round.

Eight

On the day of the fund-raiser, Allison went to Pure, the spa at The Bellamy, the same fabulous five-star resort where Allison and Rand had spent their wedding night. Megan arranged the entire thing, making sure Allison got everything the luxurious salon had to offer.

Nevertheless, Allison still fretted. Her package included a full makeover, but would it be enough to make her as glamorous as the other women attending the fund-raiser? Would it make the internet trolls sit up and take notice? Of course it wasn't just about them. She wanted to impress Rand, too.

Along with Allison, Megan was getting pampered, as well. And so was Selena Jacobs. Selena was a feisty little thing, graced with sultry features and glossy black hair. She was also Will Sanders's ex-wife—the *real* Will, not Rich Lowell.

From what Allison gathered, Selena and Will had been too young and incompatible to make their marriage work and had gotten divorced years ago. These days, she was engaged to rancher and business tycoon Knox McCoy. Although Selena and Knox had known each other since college, their friendship had just recently blossomed into love. They were even expecting a child. But the early stages of pregnancy hadn't slowed Selena down. She remained focused on her career as the creator and CEO of Clarity, a locally sourced, cruelty-free line of skin care products and cosmetics. She'd secured an exclusive deal with Pure, and today her products were being used to transform Allison.

Or so Allison hoped. For now, she was getting her hair done. She'd already had a facial, and she had to admit, the deep cleansing mask they'd applied had left her skin feeling smooth and dewy.

Rand didn't know she was at the salon. She hadn't told him that she was getting a new hairdo and having her makeup completely redone. Allison barely wore cosmetics so aside from her wholesome look at their wedding, with just traces of mascara, lip gloss and blush, Rand had never seen her glammed up.

As far as he knew, she was having lunch with Megan and Selena. But Rand was busy this afternoon, too. He was joining forces with Will to discuss the impostor case. Later, he and Allison would meet up at home and leave for the fund-raiser together.

With Megan's help, Allison had already shopped for a gown. She'd chosen a long, flowing, gold-sequined number. She hadn't shown it to Rand. She wanted to surprise him with her makeover, including the dress. This was an important night for both of them. It marked their first public appearance as husband and wife, with lots of photo opportunities. Then there was the friendly conversation they hoped to have with Ted and Sharon Marks, an exchange that could ultimately help Rand land the Brisbane deal and save his career.

Talk about pressure. Allison could barely breathe.

Struggling to relax, she gazed at herself in the mirror. A male stylist stood nearby, mixing a concoction for her hair. Megan and Selena were on either side of her, also getting their hair clipped and swooped and swirled. But they were used to preparing for glamorous parties.

Allison glanced over at Megan. She actually seemed a bit out of sorts today, quieter than usual, as if she had a lot on her mind, too.

As for Allison, she was just trying to fit into Rand's high society world without feeling like a fish out of water. She was also trying to get a grip on her relationship with him. By no means did she regret the marathon sex they'd had. If anything, she craved him more and more. More than she should. More than was natural.

It had been her idea to wait to do it again, and he'd honored her wishes. So yesterday, they hadn't touched each other at all. They hadn't even slept in the same bed. And now she wanted Rand in the worst way.

In the future, there would be no more waiting, no more hungry days or tortuous nights. The next time they made love, they would keep doing it, at least until the divorce. Regardless of how intimate they'd become, their marriage was still going to end. There was no reason to stay together. Allison would be a fool to fall in love with an untamable man.

She might be a hopeless romantic, but she wasn't going to put herself through the wringer.

When Allison fell in love, it would be with someone who wanted her to be attached to him, who wanted to be married forever. The type of guy who valued commitment, needing it as much as she did. Rand had helped her trust again, but he'd warned her time and again that he wasn't meant to be her dream man. All Rand could give her was the affair they'd embarked on.

With lots of glorious hot sex.

Rand met Will on the outskirts of town, with their vehicles parked on the side of an unpaved road. They considered getting together at the Texas Cattleman's Club in one of the private conference rooms, but they changed their minds. On this fund-raiser day, the club was besieged with activity, with caterers and florists and organizers preparing for the event, and Will couldn't take the chance of being seen by anyone who wasn't involved in the case or didn't know he wasn't dead. Since Will was lying low, he never came into the office anymore, either. So, now, whenever the two men consulted about business, it was done behind the scenes. But today they would be talking about the impostor.

Will claimed that he had lots of news to share, and Rand was eager to hear it. They stood outside of their cars, a dry summer breeze stirring the air.

Between the isolated setting and Will's dark glasses and low-brimmed hat, Rand felt as if he was in the throes of a movie with a mysterious plot. Only all of this was real.

Rand studied his friend in the harsh glare of the sun. Will had always been Royal's wonder boy, the envy of many a man and the fantasy of scores of women. Along with his family's connection to Spark Energy Solutions, he was rich and handsome and lived in the main house at the Acc in the Hole, one of the biggest and most impressive ranches in Royal. Success oozed from his blood. At thirty, he was younger than Rand by about seven years.

Today Will looked more like a ranch hand than a wealthy guy. Not only was he dressed like a cowboy, he was driving one of his ranch's work trucks. Rand was driving the luxury sedan he'd offered to Allison for the duration of their marriage. But she was still taking Uber around town.

Will said, "The DNA results from the ashes still aren't in yet. But I'll let you know as soon as they are."

Rand frowned. They had no choice but to wait for

the outcome, but he wished it would come sooner than later.

"The authorities have been following the money trail Rich left behind," Will went on to say. "There were plenty of withdrawals and transfers from before, but nothing that indicates whether he's alive or dead now. Also, I've been tracking everything he took from my personal and business accounts, but I haven't come across any purchases or investments that pin him down."

"So where did he stash all that money?" Rand thought about what Rich had stolen from Allison, as well.

"I don't know. But he ripped off the TCC, too. Since I served as treasurer and he was posing as me, he had full access to the club's accounts."

"Son of a bitch." Rand kicked a small stone beneath his shoe. "What else is going on? I can tell there's more." Will's distress seemed evident.

"It's Jason. Megan's brother." His friend blew out a hard breath. "I'm worried that he might be involved. Or he might have been victimized somehow, too. But at this point, I'm just grasping at straws."

Rand shook his head in confusion. "I don't understand. Isn't he overseas finishing up an international deal?" Jason worked for Spark Energy Solutions, too. Rand didn't know him very well on a personal level, but he certainly knew that Jason was a valuable asset to the company.

"Yes, that's where he's supposed to be. But he appears to be keeping his distance, and that isn't like him. He has a little daughter, Savannah, and he always communicates with her when he's on the road. She received some sporadic emails from him, saying that he's been off the grid and can't FaceTime with her. But that's the only explanation he gave."

"That is weird. But maybe it's the truth. Maybe he's off the beaten path and doesn't have reliable Wi-Fi. Didn't he take some extra time away from his assignment to be alone and mourn your death? That could explain why he's in a remote location. People do strange things when they're grieving."

"That's what I thought at first, too. But I've been trying to reach him with emergency calls to let him know what's going on and that I'm still alive, and he hasn't responded to me."

"Are the authorities okay with you calling him?"

Will nodded. "They agreed that I should reach out to him and see what kind of response I get. But I haven't heard from him at all."

"Have you talked to Megan about this?" Rand knew that when Megan first received the urn with Will's supposed ashes, Jason had sent her a handwritten note saying that he'd seen the body. He was the one who identified the person who died in that crash as being Will. Of course later the assumption was that he'd seen Rich's body.

"Yes, I spoke to Megan, and she's worried, too."

Rand thought about the fact that Jason hadn't come back for the funeral. Was that a bad sign? Or was he really just taking time away to mourn Will? "If Rich is still alive, then Jason sending home the ashes makes no sense. But until the results are back, there isn't much you can do but keep trying to reach Jason and hope for the best."

"I don't intend to give up. One way or another, I'm going to find out what's going on." Will lowered his sunglasses a fraction, giving Rand an intense look. "So I heard you got married." He smiled a little. "*You*. The wilding of Royal."

"What can I say? I fell in love." Rand smiled, too, even if he felt heavy inside. Will never criticized him for his lifestyle. He'd always accepted Rand for who he was, and now if there was anyone Rand hated lying to, it was Will. But he didn't have a choice. "Allison and I bonded after your funeral."

"I'm glad something good came of it," he said. "Congratulations for finding the right woman. I'm happy for you."

"Thanks. That means a lot coming from you." Even if his marriage wasn't what it seemed, he appreciated Will's support.

"You're the last guy anyone expected to settle down. But here you are, with a loyal wife by your side."

"Allison is amazing." Rand couldn't be cleaning up his image without her. She was amazing in other ways, too. He couldn't wait to get down and dirty with her again, to continue the affair they'd started. He couldn't recall wanting anyone so badly. Nor was he going to worry about how he'd "corrupted" her in bed. It wasn't as if she was going to go off the rails and become a wanton woman because of it. Allison was still the same sweet girl she'd been before they'd married. She would always have an innocence about her, as far as he was concerned. "I better go. I've got that fund-raiser later."

"I'll get back in touch when I have more news."

"I hope you hear from Jason soon."

"Me, too." Will paused. "Good luck to you and Allison."

"Thanks." They shook hands and climbed into their respective vehicles. Rand headed home, wondering if Allison was back from her lunch date yet.

When he arrived, she was in her room with the door closed. He knew enough about women not to disturb her. If she was getting ready for the fund-raiser, she probably needed time alone.

Rand got ready, too. He showered and shaved, keeping his beard stubble trimmed the way he always did. His hair was easy enough, cut in a deliberately tousled style that required minimal care.

He checked the time. He had an hour or so to spare, so he sat around in a towel and played on the internet.

Finally, he got dressed. Rand had a collection of designer formal wear to choose from.

Rather than check on Allison or knock on the doors that separated their suites, he went downstairs to wait for her. He sat in the living room like a teenager on his way to the prom.

Rand was anxious about the fund-raiser, with how many different purposes it would be serving. He wanted to get to the club a little early, if possible. Normally he was "fashionably late" to these types of events. But that was the old Rand. The new one was supposed to follow proper protocol and show up on time.

As soon as he heard Allison's footsteps coming down the stairs, he stood and smoothed his jacket. Only the moment he saw her, he couldn't speak. He just stared at her, with his mouth dumbly agape.

Who was this stunning sequined creature gliding toward him? Her hair cascaded in thick waves, with one unusually bright red streak framing the right side of her face. Her eyes were dark and smoky, and her lips were the color of Rand's favorite burgundy wine. She looked airbrushed, flawless...unreal.

A vision in gold.

He blinked to be sure he wasn't dreaming. Her gown fit her to perfection, its long, sweeping lines accentuating her curves.

She smiled. "I wanted to surprise you."

"Well, you did. You totally did. You're so damned gorgeous I don't know what to say." Everything about her was revamped, right down to her femme fatale heels and matching clutch. "I thought you were at lunch today."

"I was at Pure, the salon at The Bellamy. I asked Megan to help me prepare for the fund-raiser, and she arranged for my makeover. She also got Selena involved. The salon gave me a facial and did my makeup with her Clarity products. Selena prepared a care package for me, too, with skin care and cosmetics I can use at home. There's even a honey lip balm, softer and smoother than the one I usually wear."

She touched the streak in her hair. "Both Selena and Megan suggested that I get something dramatic done with my hair."

"What about the dress?" He couldn't get over how different she looked.

"Megan helped me shop for it. I trusted her to steer me in the right direction."

Rand wanted to steer Allison back up the stairs and straight into his big brass bed. He removed his cell phone from his pocket to take her picture. "You're going to be the talk of the town. Of the internet, too. The gossip bloggers are going to go crazy for this new look of yours. So are my followers."

She posed prettily for him. "I was hoping to get their attention. But I wanted to look good for you, too. And for myself. I always wondered what being glamorous would feel like."

"And how does it feel?" He took more pictures. She was as glamorous as a woman could be. He'd dated models and actresses and socialites who didn't compare to how breathtaking she looked right now.

"It's a bit like being Cinderella, I suppose. Except without the missing slipper or the happily-ever-after, marrying-the-prince thing." She gestured to him. "I'm already married to a hot guy." She moved closer, just inches from him. "Albeit temporarily."

He put his phone away, and suddenly he felt strange about sharing her pictures on social media. Not because he wasn't proud to show her off. But because he got the uncharacteristic urge of wanting to keep her to himself. Of course that made no sense.

He'd married Allison to change his image, and posting pictures of her was an important part of his being-tamed-by-his-wife campaign.

"Are you all right?" she asked. "You zoned out there for a minute."

"I'm fine." It wasn't as if he was actually being tamed by her. He reached around to feel for the zipper on her dress, pulling her close. "I'm stripping you bare after we get back." He already intended to make love with her tonight. He even had something special planned. "I'm peeling this right off you."

"Promise?" She slipped her arms around his waist.

"Oh, yeah." He considered kissing her, but he didn't want to mess up her lipstick. For now, he behaved like the gentleman he was supposed to be. Later, he would mess her up plenty. "I better let you go." Rand released his hold on her. He'd already taken a chance by manhandling her zipper. He knew how fragile ball gowns could be, especially the sequined variety.

"How did your meeting with Will go?" she asked.

"He filled me in on some financial stuff. But there's still no word on the DNA results."

Allison heaved a sigh. "That test seems like it's taking forever. But I guess it's just my impatience."

"Yeah, mine, too. I hate not knowing."

"Megan seemed distracted at the salon today. I figured she might be thinking about the case. But if there isn't anything new, maybe that wasn't what was on her mind."

Rand made a tight face. "She could have been

thinking about her brother, Jason." He repeated what Will had told him. "It's probably nothing to worry about. But until someone hears from Jason, there's always the possibility that something went wrong."

"Oh, how awful. I hope it turns out to be nothing."

Rand sure as hell hoped so, too. "We should get going. We have a big evening ahead of us."

"Yes, we do." Her racy red lips curved into a sensual smile. "In all sorts of ways."

Well, hot damn. Now he was back to wanting to strip her bare. "You're a tease, Mrs. Gibson."

She tossed her trendy new hair over her shoulder. "Likewise, Mr. Gibson." She walked ahead of him, en route to the garage, her stilettos clicking on the hardwood floors.

As soon as he was able, he was going to make her purr like the sex kitten she'd become. But first, they had to make an appearance at the fund-raiser.

Allison was having a grand time. The Texas Cattleman's Club was known for raising money for organizations throughout the globe, but since the Stars and Stripes fund-raiser was a patriotic celebration on the heels of an American holiday, the proceeds would be divided among United States charities that included children's hospitals and disaster relief funds.

The ballroom was decorated in red, white and blue, and a majestic bald eagle ice sculpture, representing the United States emblem, embellished the buffet. A fireworks display was scheduled for later, and she suspected it would be nothing short of spectacular.

When Allison and Rand first arrived, they sampled the food, enjoying an array of appetizers. They slow danced, too, showing everyone how blissfully in love they looked, swaying in each other's arms. But now they were mingling on their own. He was having a drink with Ted Marks, and it appeared to be going well. Allison had already socialized separately with Sharon Marks, too. In fact, they'd hit it off splendidly. As it turned out, Ted and Sharon had spent their thirtieth wedding anniversary in Ireland, where they toured the medieval castles that Sharon had been anxious to see. The Marks had also spent a few days in Kenmare, which they both adored. To Allison, that seemed like a marvelous twist of fate.

So far, this entire night had been wondrous. When she spotted Megan and Selena coming her way, she smiled. She couldn't thank them enough for her makeover.

Selena spoke first. "Well, look at you." She checked Allison out with a low whistle. "You're the belle of the ball. I'll bet your husband was drooling all over himself when he first saw you."

Allison laughed. "I did make quite an impression on him. He can't wait to get his hands on me later." She leaned in close. "And I just might let him."

Selena laughed, too. "I'll bet."

Megan stepped up and said, "The dress totally works with the hair and the makeup. It's stunning on you."

"Thank you. I couldn't have done any of this without you and Selena. You're like my fairy godmothers."

She toasted them with her club soda. She decided to skip the champagne tonight. "And speaking of beauties, you're both as gorgeous as ever." Selena wore a blazing scarlet gown, and Megan's long black silk sheath boasted jeweled accents.

After a moment's pause, Allison studied Megan a bit deeper. Did she have thoughts of her hard-to-reach brother on her mind? Allison softly said to her, "I noticed how distracted you seemed earlier, and when I mentioned it to Rand, he told me about what's going on. I hope everything turns out okay. That there's nothing to worry about."

"Thank you. You must be really astute because I was trying not to let my feelings show. I hope I didn't put a damper on your time at the salon."

"Not at all. But I was still concerned about you."

"That's so nice of you, but I'll be fine. Instead of sitting around and worrying, I decided that I'm going to be proactive and take some self-defense classes. I always wanted to learn to kick some butt, and this seems like the perfect time to do it."

Allison couldn't agree more. "Women need to empower themselves."

"Yes, we most certainly do." Megan offered a confident smile. "We need show the world what we're made of."

"Hear, hear." Selena grinned, too, and twirled the straw in her soda.

Allison found both women fascinating. Selena had always been friendly but before their trip to Pure she'd been more aloof than warm. Since Selena had fallen in love with Knox, she was opening up to more people, including Megan and Allison.

Megan and Selena certainly shared interesting backgrounds, Allison thought, with how oddly connected to Will they were. Of course, Selena was happy with Knox now, her past with Will Sanders a distant memory.

Megan was still knee-deep in Will's impostor situation. And so was Allison. Not with Will, per se, but with her marriage to Rand. In that regard, they were impostors themselves.

"I should get back to my husband," Allison said. She noticed that his chat with Ted Marks had ended, and now Rand was looking her way.

"Enjoy the rest of your evening." Megan gave Allison a sisterly hug, and she and Selena drifted into the crowd.

Allison turned toward Rand, and as they approached each other, she disposed of her empty glass. He no longer had a drink in his hand, either. As soon as they were close enough to touch, he swept her in his arms and kissed her. She sighed like a schoolgirl, immersed in the taste of him.

Afterward, he said, "I wanted to do that the moment I saw you coming down the stairs at home, but I didn't want to mess up your lipstick."

She hadn't considered her makeup, but she wasn't used to fussing over it. "Is it messed up now?"

"No. It still looks good. Did I get any of it on me?"

"A little. But I can take care of that for you." She wiped the pale red smear off him, and in that cozy moment, one of the photographers who'd been hired to cover the event took their picture. Allison didn't doubt how tender the image probably looked. But her affection for Rand had been genuine. His kiss had been real, too. They weren't being complete impostors tonight.

Once the photographer set his sights on someone else, Rand said to Allison, "Guess what I discovered about Ted?" He answered his own question. "His mother lives in the same retirement community as my grandmother."

"Really? Do you think your granny and his ma know each other?"

"We're not sure. But we plan to ask them." He reached for her hand and held it. "We should have Ted and Sharon over for a barbecue at the house. I think they would accept the invitation, and I definitely think it would be good for business."

"Then we'll do that for sure, maybe even this weekend if they're available. We can invite his ma and your granny, too. We can make it a family affair." She beamed. "I can make some traditional Irish food to go along with whatever you want to barbecue. I suspect that Sharon will want to help me. She mentioned being part of a cooking club and likes to try new recipes."

"Thanks for supporting me on this, Allison."

"You're welcome." She squeezed his hand. "It's fun being your wife." She was enjoying her role as his new socialite bride.

"You're doing a stupendous job."

"So are you. We certainly have everyone here fooled."

He glanced around the ballroom. "So who do you think are the most interesting people here, besides us?"

As Allison searched the crowd, her gaze landed on Abigail Stewart, a pretty brunette with long hair in delicately woven braids. Abigail was an accomplished artist who'd donated a critical piece to the fund-raisers for auction. She was also one of the women—along with Allison, Megan, Selena and Jillian Norris—who'd been named as an heir in the impostor's phony will.

In addition to that, Abigail had a noticeable little baby bump. With the way Rich had spread himself around, was it possible that she'd had an affair with him? That the baby was his? Jillian had already given birth to a child Rich had abandoned, so why not Abigail, too? Thankfully, Jillian was engaged to a wonderful man now, Will's stepbrother, Jesse Navarro, who was helping her raise her daughter. But Abigail appeared to be all alone.

Allison said, "I nominate Abigail Stewart as the most interesting woman here."

Rand followed her line of sight to the pregnant artist. But he didn't comment on Abigail or her condition. Instead, he asked, "What man would get your vote?"

Allison scanned the crowd again. This time, she laughed. "How about Dr. Chambers?" Vaughn Chambers was a respected trauma surgeon at Royal Me-

morial, as well as the heir to an oil fortune. But even
with as young and handsome as he was, his social
graces were sorely lacking. He looked as if he'd been
dragged to the fund-raiser by his peers. "Could he be
any more miserable?"

Rand chuckled. "Is he grumbling under his
breath?"

"It certainly seems that way to me."

"Then he gets my vote, too." A second later, Rand
went serious. "Royal is a fascinating place, isn't it?"

"Yes, it is." Allison would be returning to Dallas
when their marriage was over, but Royal was definitely making a heartfelt impression on her. She was
going to be sorry to leave it behind. Leaving Rand
behind was going to be even more painful. She would
miss everything about him. To keep from becoming
sad, she said, "I forgot to tell you that I'm officially
employed again. I received the contracts for the featured articles I told you about. The publisher emailed
them to me yesterday, and I signed them this morning and sent them off."

"Congratulations." He straightened his tie in a
businesslike manner, behaving like the CEO that he
was. "I know how much your work means to you."

"As much as yours means to you."

He moved closer to her. "We're quite the pair."

She thought about the promise he'd made to strip
her bare tonight. She stepped into his arms, pressing
her body close to his. "I'm looking forward to being
with you again."

"Me, too." He grazed her cheek with his chin. "But I think the fireworks are about to start."

She turned to see people shuffling outside. "Then I guess we better join them."

Hand in hand, they proceeded to the courtyard, the night air filled with scents of summer, fragrant flowers blooming on the club's well-tended grounds.

Still holding hands, they watched the sky explode with pops of sound and color. As magnificent as the display was, the only thing Allison could think about was going home—where she and Rand could create their own brand of fireworks.

Nine

Finally, they were home, Allison thought. Together in Rand's room, with the lights turned low and a candle burning. He claimed the candle held special powers and served a sensual purpose. The strawberries-and-cream scent did seem like an aphrodisiac. But she was already steeped in desire.

He worked her zipper and peeled off her gown, just as he'd promised to do.

"Step back so I can look at you," he commanded.

She followed his instruction, and he sat on the edge of the bed, holding her sequined garment on his lap. Aside from his jacket and shoes, he was still fully clothed.

All that remained on Allison's body was the skimpy lingerie she'd bought to go with her gown.

Rand roughly said, "Turn around. Let me see all of you."

She made a complete circle, turning slowly, and coming back to face him once again. She refused to be shy. If he wanted to look at her, then she was going to let him take his fill.

While he roamed his gaze over her, she waited for him to give her another command. She would never forget this moment, this feeling—as if she belonged to him. But she knew she couldn't let herself feel this way forever. Once their marriage ended, so would this crazy, wild affair.

"Take those off." He used his chin to motion to her undergarments.

She did his bidding. She unhooked her bra and freed her breasts. She stepped out of her pale pink thong, too.

"You're so damned beautiful," he said.

For once in her life, she felt beautiful. "This is a magical night for me." Like being in the midst of an erotic fairy tale, she thought.

He kept staring at her. "I'm letting the candle heat up. I need to be sure it's warm enough."

She glanced in the direction of Rand's mahogany bureau, where the candle sat, burning inside of a tin container. "It already smells glorious."

"I'm going to use the candle on you. I bought it for tonight to surprise you, just like you got your make-over to surprise me."

She gulped her next breath. "What do you mean you're going to *use* it on me?"

"Don't worry. It's nothing kinky. Once the wax melts, it becomes massage oil."

She gazed longingly at him, with a romantic quaver in her body, in her soul. "So you're going to pour it on me and rub it into my skin?"

"That's exactly what I'm going to do." He placed her dress on a nearby chair, then headed over to the bureau and checked the temperature of the wax, drizzling some of it onto the back of his hand.

She stood back, so wildly aroused, she could hardly breathe. The feeling of belonging to him was getting stronger. But it was just part of their affair, she reminded herself. Part of the thrill.

He extinguished the flame. "It's ready."

So was Allison, ready and willing to try a new kind of foreplay. "Should I get in bed?"

"Yes, but I need to unmake it first."

As he got rid of everything except the bottom sheet, her pulse throbbed in unmentionable places.

"Excited?" he asked.

"Yes." Just thinking about what came next was almost more than she could bear.

"I'm glad you're into it. But I figured you would be." He pointed to the bed. "Okay. Get in."

Swallowing hard, she climbed into his bed, realizing how cage-like it seemed with its brass headboard and footboard.

He came over to her with the candle. "It's the edible kind, so I can taste it, too."

She inhaled the sweet scent, inundating her senses

with it. "I should have known there was a method to your madness."

He knelt beside her, his lips curving into a randy smile.

Rand. His name filled her head. He dripped the oil onto her breasts, and she gasped in immediate pleasure, the sensation warm and sensual. He put his hands everywhere, all over her. Kneading her muscles, he gave her a luxurious massage. She moaned, and he lowered his head to flick his tongue, taking an ice cream cone–type lick right from her navel.

"Is it good?" she asked, on another moan.

"It's better than good. And now I'm going taste you where it counts, like I did before."

Except this time she would be covered in flavored oil instead of sudsy water, making it even more carnal. He lifted her legs onto his shoulders, putting her in a highly intimate position.

He used his mouth, skillful in his ministrations. Her husband, her lover, her friend; she was definitely his for the taking. She reached back, gripping the rails on the headboard.

He buried his mouth deeper, and she held the rails even tighter. He was making her wet, so incredibly wet.

By now, her entire world was centered on the heat, the pressure, the passion that overtook her. She arched her hips and rubbed against his face, participating in her orgasm.

He encouraged her to enjoy every tingle, every

shiver, every arousing tremor, and Allison came in a
stream of liquid ecstasy.

He kissed her, down there, one last time and removed his clothes, a wicked expression alight in his
eyes.

She sat up and stretched, feeling delightfully
wicked, too. She could've come a thousand times
for him.

He kissed her again, on the lips, giving her a
musky taste of herself. Such a bad boy, she thought,
such a libidinous man. She slipped away from him
and got out of bed.

"What are you doing, Allison?"

"It's my turn to seduce you." She wanted to do to
him what he'd done to her. She stood at the foot of
the bed and gestured for him to sit in front of her.

He did as he was told, even if he said, "I think I'm
in trouble."

"Yes, you are." She was going to make him beg
for mercy. She gestured to the small silver tin beside
him. "I need the candle." She noticed that the wax
was still pooling into oil.

He handed it to her, and she made a slick mess,
dripping it onto his chest in circular motions. She
poured a straight, thin line down his abs, too, where
it moved in a slow and stirring trail. Pushing his legs
apart, and being as aggressive as a determined woman
could be, she dropped to her knees in front of him.

"Holy hell," he groaned.

Hell wasn't a holy place, but she knew what he
meant. Allison roved her hands over the front of

his body, rubbing the massage oil into his skin. His erection strained, growing bigger and harder, but she didn't touch it. Not yet.

"Are you going to put your mouth on me?" he asked.

"Yes." She was going to take him all the way to the back of her throat.

He toyed with her hair, the newly highlighted strands flowing through his fingers. "Have you ever done it before?"

"Yes," she said again.

His body tensed in arousal, his hands tightening in her hair. "You never let any of your lovers do it to you, but you were doing it to them?"

"It was easier for me to give than receive." But she'd never been as brazen as she was right now. "It's going to be better with you. Deeper. As deep as I can go."

"Then do it." His voice went raspy. "Just do it."

She took her sweet time, lapping at the oil glistening on his thighs. "You taste like dessert." The strawberry stuff was yummy.

"Allison, *please*."

The begging had begun, just as she'd hoped it would. But she waited another beat before she used her mouth to drive him mad. While she took him to euphoric heights, she looked up at him, glad to see that he was watching.

Rand praised her, telling her how incredible she was, how mesmerized he was by her deep, deep throat. He cupped her chin and moved his hips to the rhythm she'd set.

She planned to keep going, to bring him to fruition, but his desire took another turn. He told her to stop, insisting that he wanted to be inside her.

She considered testing his limits, but he wouldn't let her. He dragged her up off her knees, making her as hot for him as he was for her. She fitted him with a condom and straddled his lap. He pulled her onto the bed, and with their bodies bathed in oil, they made voracious love.

He came quickly, fiercely, and so did Allison, replete with satisfaction. But she felt a bit dizzy, too, as if her heart was never going to stop spinning.

Needing to stay close to him, she cuddled in his arms and put her head on his chest. He stroked a hand down her spine, and she closed her eyes, allowing him to lull her to sleep.

On Sunday afternoon, just two days after the fundraiser, Allison and Rand hosted a barbecue. Their guests included Ted and Sharon Marks, Ted's mother, Mavis, and Rand's granny, Lottie.

The menu consisted of grilled salmon, a fresh green salad, soda bread and champ, the latter being a traditional Irish dish made with spring onions, butter, milk and mashed potatoes. Soda bread was common in Ireland, too. For dessert, they would have a light and frothy lemon pudding.

While the men drank Texas-brewed beer and fired up the grill, Mavis and Lottie chatted in the dining room, and Allison and Sharon worked side by side in the kitchen.

Allison checked on the bread, but it wasn't quite ready yet. In the old days, it used to be baked over hot coals in a covered skillet. She was making it the modern way, of course, using the oven. Earlier she'd taught Sharon how to make the champ, sharing that recipe with her.

At the moment, Sharon was in charge of the salad, creating a colorful masterpiece out of the vegetables she'd diced. She stood tall and slim in a casual blouse and ankle-cuffed linen slacks, her short blond hair perfectly coiffed. She took impeccable care of herself, wearing her fiftysomething years well.

Allison had fixed herself up, too, using the Clarity skin care products and cosmetics Selena had given her. She liked how being glamorous made her feel. She didn't want her makeover to be a onetime thing.

"It's interesting how Mavis and Lottie live in the same condominium complex and didn't even know each other until today," Sharon said, peering in the direction of the elderly women. "But it's a big place, so I can see where their paths might not have crossed."

"They certainly seem to be getting along well." Allison thought it was nice that Ted's widowed mother and Rand's never-married granny were becoming instant friends. Although Mavis was about ten years younger than Lottie, they were both former socialites living quiet lives now.

Allison checked on the bread again. This time,

she removed it from the oven and placed it on the stove top to cool.

"That smells marvelous." Sharon sniffed the air. "I loved the hearty food in Ireland. I loved everything about it."

"I'm so glad you enjoyed your trip." Allison appreciated Sharon's enthusiasm. "Rand has never been there."

"Really? He needs to see where you come from. He needs to experience it."

"We plan on renewing our vows in Kenmare next year." The lie rolled off Allison's tongue before she could take it back. And now that she'd said it, she was forced to expound. "The second ceremony will be held in the church where I was baptized."

"Oh, how lovely. You and Rand make a fascinating couple." Sharon lowered her voice. "Ted is impressed with the influence you've had on Rand. He's so different now that he's with you." Her tone returned to normal, as if she realized there wasn't any reason to whisper. They were the only two people within earshot. "It sounds like your family raised you well. I'll bet they're just the nicest people."

"Thank you. That's such a kind thing to say." The compliments made Allison feel warm and homey, even if her influence on Rand wasn't what it appeared to be. "My parents would be thrilled about how much you love Ireland. If you and Ted ever go back, I'll put you in touch with them. They love having company at the farm."

"That would be wonderful." Sharon completed the

salad, topping it with shredded cheese. "Hey, here's an idea! You can invite us to your wedding ceremony in Kenmare. It'll be a great excuse for us to return to Ireland, and we can meet your family and see the farm then."

"That's a brilliant idea." Allison embellished the lie. But what else could she do? Telling the truth wasn't an option. "A destination wedding like that will take some planning, so I should probably start compiling the guest list now." To include no one, she thought, a lump rising to her throat. By next year, she and Rand would be long-since divorced.

When it was time to eat, they sat outside, enjoying the weather. During the meal, Rand and Ted talked sports. Both men were golfers with similar handicaps.

"Kenmare has a famous old golf course," Allison said, joining the conversation. Since the gated community where Rand lived was a golfer's haven, she wanted everyone to know that her hometown had a golf club, too.

Ted jumped in and excitedly said, "I golfed there." He proceeded to tell Rand it was one of most scenic courses he'd ever had the pleasure of playing, with its breathtaking views of the Irish countryside.

Suddenly Allison wished that she and Rand really would be going to Ireland together next year. But her wish made no sense. What were they supposed to do while they were there? Hang out as a divorced couple?

After the afternoon wound down, everyone went home except for Rand's grandmother. She wanted to stay and visit a bit longer. Instead of returning to the patio, they gathered in the living room, sipping mint-flavored iced tea and eating second helpings of dessert. Allison and Rand sat side by side on the sofa, while his granny took a wingback chair.

Lottie was an elegant sight to behold, with her snow-white hair, fragile skin and deep blue eyes. Pinned to the lapel of her blouse was a red garnet brooch. It looked like an antique piece, probably purchased from the same jeweler who'd provided Allison's engagement and wedding rings.

They chatted about inconsequential things, until Lottie said to Allison, "I'm aware that my short-term memory is failing. I know that I'm being treated for it. But it's strange because I can't really tell how bad it is. When you're the one it's happening to, you don't remember that you're being forgetful."

"I can only imagine how difficult that must be," Allison replied. "To have other people reminding you of what you're supposed to remember."

Lottie dipped into her pudding, stirring it with her spoon. "At my age, I'm lucky I still have all of my other faculties. But you know what? I remember my past. I remember when Rand's mother died. She was my only child, and I loved her dearly. I remember raising Rand and Trey and how much joy they gave me." She quietly added, "And I remember the feeling of being in love."

Allison's heart thudded in her chest, and she glanced at Rand to get his reaction. He met her gaze, then returned his attention to his grandmother, letting her speak her emotional piece.

Lottie continued by saying, "His name was Eduardo Ruiz, and he was the love of my life and the father of my child. But I knew it would never work between us. That he was incapable of returning my love. I used to think that Rand had inherited Eduardo's restless spirit. That he was just like him. But he isn't." Lottie spoke directly to him. "You wouldn't have married Allison if you were like him. You wouldn't have fallen in love with her."

Rand closed his eyes, as if he was summoning the courage to reaffirm his deception. When he opened them, he said, "You're right, Grandma. I'm not who I used to be. My wife changed me."

Lottie quickly replied, "Then you should tell her about your grandfather. The entire story. She's part of our family now, and she should know how deeply it affected you when you first learned about him. You should show her the pictures I gave you of him, too." She said to Allison, "The resemblance between them is uncanny."

"I'm looking forward to hearing more about him and seeing his pictures," Allison replied, curious to make the comparison herself. "Rand already mentioned him briefly to me. He was cautious about saying too much because he was protecting your privacy."

Lottie sighed. "I've always kept Eduardo close to my heart. He was a secret I preferred not to share, except with my grandsons. I probably wouldn't have even told them if Rand hadn't bore such a strong likeness to him." After a light pause, she sighed again.

"Eduardo was wrong for me. But Rand isn't wrong for you. Just seeing the two of you, so much in love, fills me with gladness."

Allison's chest went tight. She sensed Rand's discomfort, too. But as usual, they carried on their charade, behaving like the newlyweds they were supposed to be. He even reached for her hand, threading his fingers through hers.

"You're living my dream," Lottie said. "You and Rand."

No, they weren't, Allison thought. But she smiled as if they were, holding much too tightly to Rand's hand. Earlier, she'd gotten sidetracked by a second wedding ceremony in Ireland that wasn't going to happen, and now Rand's granny was pulling her into the fray, too.

Making Allison wonder how it would feel to fall in love with Rand for real.

At bedtime, Allison tried not to fret about her wayward thoughts. She was a romantic, after all, an aspiring novelist with a curious imagination. She was bound to have weak moments. But the fact that she'd actually entertained the notion of loving her husband presented a fear she hadn't intended to face.

Rand emerged from the bathroom. He'd already brushed his teeth and stripped down to his underwear, but he'd yet to get into bed with her. They were in his suite, amid his belongings. He hadn't invited her to move into his room, and she didn't expect him to. Lovers or not, they still had separate accommodations.

"Are you all right?" he asked. "You seem preoccupied."

"I'm fine." If she had another bout of weakness, she would simply will it away. Surely she was strong enough to do that.

He gave her an uncertain look. "Are you sure?"

Instead of insisting on how dandy she was, she turned the conversation around on him. "You seem distracted, too. You haven't even told me about your grandfather yet."

"I was waiting until you were settled in for the night."

"Then I'm ready now." After the emotional day she'd had, she was as settled as she was going to be.

"I'll go get Eduardo's pictures." He proceeded to his walk-in closet and returned with a small wooden keepsake box.

He joined her in bed, opened the box and showed her a head-and-shoulders photograph of a man dressed in an intricately embellished gold jacket, like that of a matador.

"Oh, my goodness." She studied the image. "Your resemblance to him *is* uncanny." There were differences, of course. Eduardo had brown eyes instead of green. He was also leaner than Rand, with cheekbones that arched higher and sharper. He wore his hair slicked straight back and was clean shaven. Beard stubble wasn't a trend in the 1950s, which she presumed was the era of the picture. But overall, they bore strikingly similar features, with the same straight noses, flared nostrils, dark eyebrows, sexy mouths and strong jawbones. "You told me before that he was really famous in his country. A bullfighter, I presume?" Based on his ceremonial clothes, she figured that was an accurate guess.

"He was from Spain, and he was legendary in his field. Not only for his performance in the ring, but because of his brash behavior in public, too. Eduardo was an illegitimate descendant of a Spanish duke, who was the half brother of a long-ago king."

She widened her eyes. "That's quite a legacy."

"In theory, it was. Except by then, Spain was being ruled by a military dictator with no ties to Eduardo's ancestors. Of course, his illegitimate connection to royalty wouldn't have awarded him that status even if they were still in power. But he liked to flaunt his lineage anyway, especially to the current regime."

"What a brave thing to do." She doubted that the dictator in charge appreciated being called out by a daring young matador.

"Everything about him seemed larger than life. He even died in a dramatic way, getting gorged by a bull and dying in the ring, with a crowd of people watching."

"That's horrible." She couldn't fathom seeing something like that. "How old was he when he died?"

"Around my age. It happened about ten years after his affair with my grandmother. They were both in their twenties when they had their fling." Rand removed another photo from the box. "Here's a snapshot of them together."

She took the picture and held it up to the light. "Your granny was beautiful." Lottie had been a leggy brunette back then, with smooth, fair skin and a bewitching smile. "She could've been a movie star. They made a stunning couple. They look really good together."

"He looked good with lots of women. He was a renowned playboy. You heard what Grandma said about him being the wrong man for her. She knew better than to try to pin him down."

Although Allison was compelled to know more, she tried not to think about the parallels between his grandparents and her relationship with Rand. "How did they meet?"

"She was on an extended holiday in Europe, traveling by herself and learning about other cultures. On her second day in Spain, she attended one of his bullfights. It's customary for people to toss flowers and gifts into the ring, and she tossed a bouquet of red roses at his feet. She was seated very close, and he noticed her in the stands and bowed to her. That's not something a matador is supposed to do. Or it wasn't in those days. I don't know about now. They weren't supposed to look around or show their fans favor. But Eduardo had become notorious for choosing his lovers that way."

Allison envisioned the scenario in her mind, the power of Eduardo's effect on the women he took to his bed. "And that's how their affair began?"

Rand nodded. "He introduced himself to her after the fight, and she spent the rest of that summer with him at his estate. She didn't speak Spanish, but he spoke fluent English, so there wasn't a language barrier. He was proficient in French, too."

"It sounds like he valued his education."

"He definitely did. He was impressed with my grandmother's alma mater in the States. Her beauty and intelligence fascinated him. He was devoted to her during the time they were together. She said that he doted on her. But he never stayed with anyone longer than a few months. That's pretty much my record, too." He took the photo of his grandparents and set it aside. "Eduardo was a wealthy man. Even when Spain was suffering economically, he managed to rise to the top. He enjoyed being a celebrity and thumbing his nose at authority."

She mulled over Rand's character, and Eduardo's, too. "Sort of like the way you thumbed your nose at Texas society to get back at your dad? I can see why Lottie thought that you inherited Eduardo's restless spirit."

"It bothers me that she thinks I've changed. I know I shouldn't be upset by it. The whole idea was to clean up my image and fool everyone into believing that we're a committed couple." A hard frown creased Rand's forehead. "But I'm still the same man I was before, and this ruse of ours isn't going to change me."

Allison didn't want to think too deeply about Rand's unchanged ways, so she focused on his grandfather instead. "I'll bet Eduardo would have married

Lottie if he'd known about the baby." She wanted to believe the best of Eduardo.

"I agree. He probably would've. Wild as he was, he was still raised in a traditional family. But that was a factor in why my grandmother didn't tell him she was pregnant. She didn't want him marrying her out of duty and resenting her for it. She didn't want a husband who would be mourning his freedom."

She couldn't help herself from saying, "But maybe it wouldn't have been that way. Maybe he would have fallen in love with her."

Rand scowled. "What are you doing, Allison? Trying to rewrite my grandfather's story and make him into one of your book heroes?"

"It's better than the way it turned out, with your granny raising a daughter all by herself and Eduardo dying so young."

"I'm sorry that he was killed the way he was, but he knew the risks he was taking. To be honest, I don't believe in bullfighting. I think it's a brutal practice."

She didn't approve of the tradition, either, but Eduardo's passing still made her sad. "Maybe he would have quit his profession if he'd married Lottie. He obviously had plenty of money to start over in the States. Between the two of them, they could've had a nice, safe life here in Texas."

Rand blew out a breath. "Do you honestly think Eduardo would still be alive if he and my grandmother had stayed together?"

"I'd like to think it could've happened." She wanted to reunite Lottie with the man she'd loved, if only in a make-believe way. It was certainly safer than daydreaming about herself and Rand.

He adjusted his weight on the bed. "You really are a hopeless romantic."

"I always said that I was." Denouncing that side of her personality would be futile.

He toyed with the strap on her nightgown, lowering it, letting it drop below her shoulder. "You look different now, with the way you changed your makeup and hair. But you're still the same person deep inside."

"Yes, I'm still the same me." The same woman who believed in happily-ever-after, who was supposed to find her true husband someday. But it was impossible to think about her future, about marrying someone else, when she was here with Rand.

"Let's see if you taste as sweet as you always have." He kissed her, soft and slow.

She returned his affection, eager to breathe him into her pores. There was no time to think, to be rational; all she could do was react. Once they were naked, their bodies entwined, he looked into her eyes. She tried to glance away, but she couldn't. He was holding her captive, making her want him even more. But as enticing as he was, she knew how important it was to keep her heart intact.

So even when he was inside of her, so close and deep that she could barely distinguish her heartbeat from his, she kept fighting her feelings.

Every silky, sexy moment of the way.

Ten

The following day, Allison continued to manage her feelings, reminding herself that her marriage to Rand wasn't meant to last. That he wasn't her true husband. That she wasn't destined to spend the rest of her life with him.

But she would miss him terribly when it was over. He was fast becoming the person she felt closest to in this world, a dear friend, a passionate lover, a kind and caring confidant, everything she always dreamed a real husband should be. But that didn't mean she could allow herself to love him. She simply had to stay strong and stop her romantic notions from taking over. Rand made it clear that he was still the same uncommitted man he'd always been.

Luckily, other things were falling into place that

she didn't have to worry about. The social media feed-back about her makeover was positive, and she was busy researching and writing the featured articles in her current contracts.

She sat at the dining room table, a soothing breeze coming in from a set of etched glass doors, and tapped away on her laptop. It was one of her favorite spots in the house. The pool was visible from her vantage point, the water glistening like a blue lagoon.

Rand was at the office, but she'd received a text from him, saying that he would be home shortly. He had some great news to share, except he wanted to wait to tell her in person. He also told her not to fix anything for dinner. Instead, they would go out to-night to celebrate.

For now, she snacked on corn chips and salsa. Al-lison had a habit of eating at her computer, and some-times she made a mess. But she was trying not to do that today. She shoved the chips into her mouth as quickly as she scooped them into the salsa bowl, keeping her laptop out of the line of fire.

About fifteen minutes later, Rand entered the house. She heard the familiar sound of his footsteps. She turned around in her chair, preparing to greet him.

He approached her, looking like the handsome young CEO that he was. His blue-striped, classic-cut suit fit him to perfection. His megawatt smile was perfect, too. This wonderful man she wasn't al-lowing herself to love.

Determined to keep things light, she stood and

teasingly said, "Hey, sugar. How was your day?" using a really bad Texas accent. But at least she had on the right clothes to fit her voice. She was wearing her one-and-only pair of cowboy boots.

He laughed. "Seriously? You're poking fun at the way I talk, and you won't let me say 'top of the morning' to you? How is that fair?"

She moved closer to him, keeping the silly banter going. "Then go ahead and say it."

"I would, but it's not morning." He swept her into his arms, bending her backward for a steamy kiss.

Mercy, she thought. Morning, noon or night, she savored the feel of him. He ended the kiss, righted their postures and let her go. Still spellbound, she gazed into the glittering greenness of his eyes.

"You taste spicy," he said.

And he tasted like heaven on earth. "It's the peppers in the salsa I ate. You know how I like to snack." She dusted her hands on her jeans, just in case she had salt from the chips on them.

He removed his jacket and draped it over the back of the chair she'd been using. "Do you want to hear my news?"

"Yes, of course." She was interested to know what they would be celebrating tonight.

He grinned broadly. "I met with Ted today and acquired the Brisbane account. I brought his company in as a new client."

"Congratulations!" She'd never seen him so boyish and smiley. She considered flinging her arms around him, but his kiss had already knocked her for a loop.

He loosened his tie. "It wouldn't have happened without you. You're my good luck charm."

She definitely felt a part of it, with how friendly they'd both become with Sharon and Ted. "I was glad to help."

"Now all we have to do is get you your green card, and our final mission will be accomplished."

A final mission that would end in divorce, she thought, with no more kisses, no more hugs, no more husband and wife.

If only things could be different, if only…

"So what are you in the mood to eat?" he asked. "Where should we go?"

Trying to clear her head, she made an instant decision. "Mexican food and margaritas sounds good."

"Really? After the chips and spicy salsa you just munched on?"

She nodded. "That's what got me in the mood for it."

"There's a really great Tex-Mex place in town. Will that do?"

"Sure." She didn't care if it was Tex-Mex or traditional Mexican cuisine. She just needed to go out and have a good time, to be as upbeat as possible.

He smiled once again. Not as boyishly as before, but still a little crookedly. "I'll change into something casual, and we can head out."

She nodded and smiled, too. "No hurry. I have to go to my room to get my purse." Just as she reached for her smartphone, so she could take it upstairs and put it in her purse, the device rang. It was on the table, next to her laptop.

Rand said, "You can let it go to voice mail and deal with it later."

"Let me check to see who it is first. It could be my agent with a mega book deal." She was joking, naturally. But someday, she intended to get that call. She glanced at the name on the screen. "It's my brother. I should probably take it." Rhys rarely called her.

She answered with a goofy "Howdy," using her ridiculous Texas accent on him.

"Allison? Is that you?" He sounded worried.

"Yes, it's me." She turned serious. His reaction to her joke was alarming. Normally Rhys had a good sense of humor. Or with her, he typically did. "Is something wrong?"

"Granny had a stroke. We don't know if she's going to recover. We don't—"

"Oh, dear God." Her knees nearly buckled, the fear of losing her grandmother flooding her like a storm. "I'll be there as soon as I can." Allison wasn't supposed to return to Ireland, not while her green card interview was pending, but this would be considered an emergency. She needed to go home.

Her brother replied, "I'll keep in touch. Be safe and let me know when you'll arrive."

"I will. I'll talk to you later." She had to figure out her traveling plans. She turned toward Rand. He'd been watching her with a concerned expression.

"What happened?" he asked.

"It's Granny. *Maimeó*," she said, using the Irish term, before she burst into tears.

Rand used his private jet to take Allison and himself to Ireland. He wasn't going to let her go alone—he wanted to be with her, to support her, to help her through this difficult time. Once he freed up his schedule, he contacted the USCIS to let them know that Allison needed to return to her homeland for a family illness. The two of them both breathed a sigh of relief when she was granted permission to leave the States.

They arrived at Kerry Airport and rented a car. Allison's grandmother was in a nearby hospital. The town of Kenmare, which was located in Kerry County, was a bit farther. But for now, they were headed directly to the hospital.

While Rand drove, Allison kept in constant touch with her family. She'd texted them from the plane, too. So far, the status of her grandmother's condition hadn't changed. She was still in critical condition.

Allison looked tired and worried and frazzled, more vulnerable than he'd ever seen her. He would be in a state of fear, too, if it was Lottie who'd fallen ill.

"This isn't how I envisioned your first trip to Ireland," Allison said to him, "if you ever came here at all."

"This isn't something I could've imagined, either." Not with someone in her family being in jeopardy. As far as Rand knew, her grandmother, Fiona, was seventy-eight years old and had been in excellent health up until now. No doubt Allison's grandfather, Cormac, was a nervous wreck. He and Fiona had been married for over fifty years. Rand couldn't fathom losing someone who'd been in your life that long. He prayed silently that Fiona recovered. Allison had prayed openly on the plane, using Celtic rosary beads that her grandma had given her when she was a child.

The hospital, a series of white brick-and-glass buildings, was only fifteen minutes away. Rand parked, and they rushed inside and got directions to the unit where her grandma was. He held Allison's hand as they dashed down sterile hallways.

The family was gathered around Fiona's bed. Cormac sat beside his wife, keeping a loving vigil. Amid the starched white sheets, Fiona appeared small and weak, with her cap of matted white hair, pale complexion and IVs taped to her arms.

Allison's distraught parents, Sheila and Angus, took turns hugging their daughter. They hugged Rand, too. When Rhys approached them, Allison put her head on her brother's shoulder. He was a solid wall of a man, as big and strong as could be, with short, medium brown hair and light brown eyes. After he comforted his sister, he shook Rand's hand and thanked him for coming.

Allison approached the bed and stood next to her grandfather's chair. Rand held back and watched the scene unfold.

Sheila came over to him and said, "Allison's granny is getting the best care possible. She was treated immediately, and her doctor told us how important that is. But I think having Allison here is going to be the best medicine of all."

He glanced at Fiona. She definitely seemed aware that her beloved granddaughter was by her side now. But there still wasn't anything any of them could do, except continue to pray as they'd been doing all long.

By the next day Fiona's condition was upgraded to stable, and if her progress continued the way it was, she would be transferred to a rehabilitation center in the area. For now, she still had some residual effects from the stroke. But overall, she was doing much better. To Rand, it felt like nothing short of a miracle, and on this picturesque afternoon while everyone else was visiting Fiona, he was at the farm with Allison's brother.

Typically, July was the driest month in Kenmare with mild temperatures, although it could turn cool and damp without warning. Either way, Rhys had put Rand to work on the farm. Rhys claimed that he was shorthanded and needed extra help, but Rand suspected that he was being "tested" to see how he measured up.

Cartwright Farms owned hundreds of sheep and baby lambs. Just this morning, Rhys had taught Rand how to shear sheep—with a pair of hand shears. Most farmers used machines these days, but the Cartwrights still did it the old, traditional way. They thought machines took off too much wool, also leaving the sheep too cold afterward. Sheep could be shorn in all seasons, depending on the location and the conditions. Here, it was a summer activity.

As hard as the work was, Rand was invigorated by it. Although he'd always enjoyed being outdoors, he'd never known anything quite like this. It felt good being part of something so real, something that didn't involve taking selfies and promoting himself online. The influence of Allison's homeland was putting Rand in an authentic state of mind. Would he feel this way once he returned to Texas, too? Would he start living a more private life? He'd already gotten a little weirded out on the night of the fund-raiser about sharing pictures of Allison. He'd actually wanted to keep her to himself.

Before he taxed his mind too deeply about that, he returned his attention to the farm. At the moment, he and Rhys were taking a break, away from the barn where they'd shorn the first group of sheep.

Rhys stood near a fence rail. A black-and-white border collie, a National Champion Sheepdog finalist, sat loyally at his feet. Beyond man and dog were acres and acres of lush green valleys, surrounded by natural brush, low hills and high mountains.

Rand said, "If my father could see me now, he would accuse me of just playing in the dirt. He didn't think I was good for anything."

"I'm rather surprised myself," Rhys replied. "I didn't expect you to take to this so easily. But you do look as if you've been rolling around in the dirt."

"Maybe because I have?" The first few sheep Rand had tried to shear had knocked him on his butt.

"There are tons of ranches where I come from, and some of my closest friends are renowned horse breeders and cattlemen, but I was raised in a luxurious mansion that my grandmother used to own."

"Then you're doing all right for a spoiled rich boy." Rhys chuckled, flashing what could only be described as a lethal smile.

"Gee, thanks." Rand swigged his water.

Silent, Rhys rubbed his hand across his jaw. He had the kind of beard scruff that made him look tough, not trendy. But as rugged as he was, he was a savvy businessman, too. His London-based company, Cartwright News and Media, was highly successful.

"Have you always taunted Allison's beaus?" Rand asked. "Or were you just reserving it for me?"

"I've done far worse to some of the lads she dated. But she isn't dating you." Rhys squinted at him. "If you weren't already married to her, I would probably be hounding you about your intentions, making sure they were honorable."

Rand's guilt reared its head. *Honorable* wasn't a word that applied to the reasons he'd married Allison. Sure, he'd accompanied her to Ireland to see her ailing grandmother, but that didn't change the dynamics of their phony marriage.

"She seems happy with you," Rhys added.

Now the big Irishman was being brotherly, heightening Rand's guilt. Allison deserved better; all of the Cartwrights did. Rand wasn't the man her family thought he was. His divorce to Allison was imminent. But even as the thought crossed his mind, a sense of loneliness came over him. He was getting used to being her husband.

Her *fraudulent* husband, he reminded himself. He didn't know the first thing about being a loyal partner, and he never would. It simply wasn't in his DNA. The grandfather he favored was a party boy, and even Rand's own father, with his high-and-mighty attitude, had been a terrible husband—and not just to Rand's mother. His dad had been married four times in total, with each of his screwed-up marriages ending in divorce.

"When Allison gets back, you two should go into town," Rhys said, cutting into Rand's troubled thoughts. "With everything else that's been going on you haven't gotten the chance to see the sights. She can show you the church where your convalidation is going to take place next year. That's going to be a major event around here. So you might as well start gearing up for it now."

The last thing Rand wanted was to visit the site where his marriage to Allison was supposed to be blessed. To keep his anxiety in check, he made a joke. "Maybe you and I ought to go out for a pint of Guinness instead."

Thankfully, Rhys laughed. "I'll take you pub hopping another time. For today, you should go to Holy Cross. You and Allison can light a candle for Granny while you're there."

"Then that'll be the plan." Rand certainly couldn't refuse. Even if he was no longer a churchgoer, he still believed in the power of prayer. But pretending to her family that he and Allison were going to renew their vows in a sacred ceremony was another matter.

"Come on." Rhys gestured in the direction of the barn. "We've got more work to do before either of us can go anywhere."

Rand nodded, clearing the emotional tension from his mind and returning his focus to the farm.

Later that afternoon, Rand sat across from Allison in a secondhand bookstore that doubled as a vegetarian café and organic produce market, eating biscuits and soup.

He learned that she used to come here often. Writer that she was, she loved being surrounded by used books, immersing herself in the essence of how they looked and felt and smelled. He enjoyed the setting, too. Rand liked everything about Kenmare. The Irish name for it was Neidín, meaning little nest. He thought it fit the town beautifully, with how charmingly it was nestled against the mountains. In addition to its quaint atmosphere, Kenmare was also known for scenic walks, offering short jaunts or long-distance routes, along the peninsulas or through the hills.

"It's almost as if time stands still here," he said. "I've traveled to lots of places, to many countries and continents, but nothing has affected me like this."

"I'm so glad you're here with me." Allison took a sip of her soup. Afterward, she said, "And to think that Rhys has been teaching you to work the farm." She grinned. "Who knew that you'd be so good at it?"

Rand slathered his biscuit with almond butter. "I was trying not to look like a fool in front of him. Your brother is one tough dude."

"And I'm one tough gal." She waved her spoon at him. "Remember how I kicked your arse during our football and rugby match back in Texas?"

He rolled his eyes, but he smiled, too. "How could I forget?" His losing that game had been the start of their affair.

She lowered her spoon. "I can relax now that Granny is getting better. I was so worried about her. I can't even…"

Her words drifted, but he understood what she was trying to convey: the fear, the possibility of losing her grandmother. But everything was going to be okay now.

He reached across the table for her hand, and the tips of their fingers touched.

She asked, "When we leave here, do you want to see the restaurant where I used to work? Not to eat there since we're already eating, but just to have me point it out?"

"Sure." He wanted to become more familiar with her past. But even so, the reminder of the restaurant bothered him. He knew it was where she'd met Rich Lowell, and now Rand was beginning to wonder if he was being as unscrupulous as Rich. Even if he wasn't lying to Allison about his identity or plotting to steal her money, he was conning her family, doing whatever he could to earn their admiration and respect.

But his biggest issue was Allison herself. What if he broke her heart when their marriage was over?

She'd promised that she wasn't going to get attached to him, and he'd taken her at her word. But could a hopeless romantic like Allison truly keep a promise like that? Was it only a matter of time before she developed feelings for him that weren't part of their deal? Even now, she was giving him a tender look. A wifely look, he thought.

Well, of course she was, he relented. She was supposed to act like that when they were in public. He was probably giving her goo-goo eyes, too. It was a habit they'd both formed.

But still, there was something about the way she was behaving that gave him pause. It just felt different, somehow.

They finished their soup and biscuits and proceeded to the restaurant where Allison used to work.

"It gets lots of tourist business," she said, as they stood in front of the colorfully painted building.

"It looks like a nice place. But it makes me think of Rich being here with you." He couldn't seem to stop himself from admitting that her affair with Rich had crossed his mind.

"He only came into the restaurant when we were first getting to know each other. Once we started dating, we were careful not to be seen in town together. It's crazy now that I think back on it. I should have known that no good would come of a relationship I was hiding from my family."

"We're hiding things about our relationship from

your family, too. And mine and everyone else we know."

"At least neither of us is married to someone else."

Yes, but were the circumstances of their marriage any less deceptive? Rand hardly thought so. "Your brother wants you to show me the church where our second ceremony is supposed to take place."

"He mentioned it to me, as well. But he assumed I would want you to see it." She paused. "I hope you don't mind going there. I agree with him that we should light a candle for Granny."

"I think we should, too." Rand was already prepared to do that.

Since Holy Cross was within walking distance, they continued on foot.

As they approached the building, he stopped to study the Gothic Revival–style architecture, with its gray-and-white stone exterior, pitched slate roofs, corner buttresses and stunning stained glass windows. A large, freestanding Celtic cross was part of the design, too.

"It's a beautiful church," he said, realizing that Allison's family had probably worshipped here for generations. "Do you know when it was consecrated?"

"It was in 1864, but the local land agent didn't want to provide a site for it. In fact, the priest who built it topped the spire with a weather vane rooster. Everyone around here thinks it's because he wanted the rooster to crow over the pernickety agent. The agent's office used to be located in the town square."

She gestured in the direction of where the agent had supposedly been crowed upon.

Rand laughed. "Now, that's my kind of priest."

She laughed, as well. "Mine, too." After a breath of serious silence, she asked, "Do you want to go inside now?"

"Not yet." He needed to talk to her first. "Remember when I told you that I hadn't been to church in a really long time? I never explained why I stayed away, and I want to do that now."

She met his gaze. "I'm listening, Rand. You can say whatever feels right."

At this point, he didn't know what felt right, but he started at the beginning. "My grandmother didn't raise me in this faith. Neither did my father. But my mother did. She joined the church after she and Dad got divorced. Mom had me baptized, and I used to like going to mass with her. But after she died, that part of my life ended." He hesitated before he said, "When I was old enough to attend services by myself, I returned to the parish where she used to take me. But it wasn't the same. It just reminded me of my mother's funeral and how painful it had been to lose her. So I stopped going, and I haven't been back since."

"I'm so sorry." She made a soft sound. "Did it help to stay away?"

"No. The pain was still there." He glanced at the arched doorways, leading to the entrance of the church. "I'd like to light a candle for my mother while we're here. I think she would've loved this place."

Allison's eyes went misty. "I'll bet she's watching over us right now."

He let out the breath he was holding, releasing it from his lungs. "I hope so."

They entered the building, and Allison dipped into the holy water, making the sign of the cross in front of her. Rand did, too, with his childhood memories flooding back. Good memories, he thought, of when his mom was alive.

The interior was even more impressive, light and airy with a high marble altar, decorative floors and carved wooden ceilings, rife with angels.

They approached the alcove and lit two candles, one for her grandmother and another one for his mother. After they spent some quiet time in prayer, Rand glanced over at Allison and wondered what renewing their vows here would be like.

A second later, he shook away the thought. One peaceful moment in a big, beautiful Irish church didn't mean that he was meant to stay with Allison. Nor did it make him the kind of husband she needed. If anything, it just solidified the fact that she deserved more than he was capable of giving her.

When they returned to Texas, he was going to do everything within his power to get the green card interview moved up, hastening her opportunity to start a new life.

Without him.

Eleven

On Allison and Rand's third and final day in Ireland, the weather turned cool and windy. They would be flying back to Texas that evening, but for now they were on a long and winding walk through the hills. For Allison, the trail was wonderfully familiar. She was taking Rand to see her childhood hideaway.

He asked, "How much farther is it?"

"We're getting closer." The location was adjacent to the farm, but still on Cartwright property.

He glanced around. "The scenery is breathtaking. It's wonderful how well your grandmother is doing, too."

Allison nodded. She was extremely grateful for Granny's prognosis. "She certainly likes you." When they visited her this morning, she called him, "A prince from a land called Royal."

"I'll bet she was a flirt in her day."

"Yes, she was." But Ma swooned over him, too. She was even knitting him a sweater with wool from the farm, promising to send it to him. Da, Granda and Rhys were impressed with Rand, as well. He'd passed their inspections with flying colors.

As for Allison, she'd finally given up the fight. She was no longer battling her feelings. Somewhere in the midst of this emotionally charged trip, she'd fallen madly, irreversibly in love with Rand.

But love was a good thing, a beautiful thing, and she refused to regret that it had happened to her. She needed to be hopeful, to work toward keeping the man she loved instead of dwelling on the idea of losing him.

But even with her newfound confidence, she was still afraid, doubt and worry creeping in. He'd told her countless times he couldn't be tamed. That he was the same man he'd always been. Yet now that she'd fallen in love with him, she wanted to believe otherwise. With as wonderful a husband as he was—how could she not think that he'd changed?

Before her brain got too befuddled, she pointed to the final hill they had to cross. "We're almost there. It's just beyond that ridge."

"So what exactly is this hideaway of yours?"

"It's just some lovely old ruins." She didn't want to give him too much detail, not until he saw it for himself. "When I was a girl, I used to think of it as my fort. And when I was a teenager, it's where I used to come to write poems to my fantasy husband."

The wind rustled his hair. "Ah, yes, those secret poems. It's too bad you didn't keep them."

It wouldn't matter if she still had them. She already knew that Rand Gibson had emerged from her fantasies, becoming the man of her heart.

After they trudged over the final hill and he spotted her hideaway, an awed expression appeared on his handsome face. Allison felt that way every time she saw it, particularly at this time of year when it was surrounded by wildflowers.

He said, "I would have used this as my fort, too. It's incredible."

"It's called a beehive hut because of the rounded way it's shaped. No windows, nothing but an opening that serves as a door. But you can see how small the opening is, so it can easily be covered with one larger stone." She explained further, "It's a prehistoric home, a single-family dwelling of sorts. There's a little community of these in another part of Kerry County, where the huts were once attached to each other through interlocking doorways. But on our land, there's just this one."

Rand approached the structure and glided his hands along the exterior. "Look at the way each stone is stacked and how they're angled outward. Was that so the rain could run off it?"

Allison nodded. "Do you want to duck inside?"

"Definitely." He gestured for her to go first. "I'll follow you in."

She warned him by saying, "It's going to be dark in there, except for the bit of light that comes through the opening. But with as small as the hut is, there isn't much to explore inside. Still, I used to carry a battery-operated lantern with me when I came here."

He smiled. "So you could sit and write your poems by the lantern light? I can just see you doing that, all alone in your make-believe world."

Was she tumbling into a make-believe world now, imagining happily-ever-after with him? Focusing on her task, she crawled into the hut.

He joined her, and they sat near the opening. He said, "I can't fathom living in one of these. But it's a perfect hideaway."

She peered out at the flowers scattered in the grass. "It served me well."

"It's serving us well, too."

He leaned over to kiss her, and she sighed. The child in her had grown up, but the starry-eyed teenager she used to be had never gone away.

"Can I touch you?" he asked.

She knew he meant in a sexual way, doing more than a soft, sweet kiss. "Yes," she breathed. As far as she was concerned, he could touch her for the rest of their lives.

"I'll just use my hands." He lifted her onto his lap, with her sitting with her back to his front. He nuzzled the side of her face and unzipped her jeans.

She closed her eyes, and he worked his right hand past the waistband of her knickers. With his left hand, he unbuttoned the front of her rugged plaid blouse.

He cast an erotic spell, making her nipples peak, causing dampness to pool between her thighs. She leaned back against him, the long-ago poems she'd written twirling in her mind. She'd found her fantasy husband. He'd become real.

He whispered, "I'm never going to forget you, Allison."

She opened her eyes and gazed into a darkened corner of the hut. He sounded as if he were saying goodbye. "We're still together, Rand."

"I know. But I just wanted to tell you how special you are for when we're not together anymore."

She refused to accept his words. "We still have lots of time." Time, she prayed, for her to keep him.

He didn't reply. Instead, he went farther into her knickers.

She grabbed ahold of his blue-jeaned thighs, scratching her nails along the denim. He seemed hell-bent on making her come. But what choice did she have?

She lifted her hips and pressed against his fingers, the sensation of being seduced by him igniting its way to her lovelorn heart. The more he aroused her, the more she wanted, the more she needed. Allison climaxed hard and quick, wrapped in her husband's arms.

Both Allison and Rand slept on the plane, and the next day they were back in Texas and returning to work. She noticed that he seemed pensive, far quieter than his usual self. He was dressed for the office, sipping coffee and gazing out the patio doors.

She stood behind him, with her laptop on the table. She had her articles to write.

He finally turned toward her and said, "We have our green card interview tomorrow."

She staggered as if she'd been shot. "Tomorrow? How is that even possible? It's too soon. It must be a mistake."

"No, it's not. I contacted my friend at the USCIS to see how things were going and if he could push things along even more than he already had."

Allison knew that Rand's friend had gotten her security clearance processed faster and was working toward getting their interview date moved up. But she hadn't envisioned anything this quick. "I figured we were at least a month off." Even that would have been quicker than the usual expected wait time. "How did he manage it?"

"Mostly it was timing and luck. When he checked the books, he discovered that another couple had canceled, so he moved us up the line and arranged for us to take their slot. He faxed me the notification this morning. He sent the original, too, overnight, so it'll arrive first thing in tomorrow's mail."

To her, this was the worst thing that could've happened. Getting her green card sooner meant their marriage would end sooner. How could she try to hold on to Rand if they weren't married anymore? "We can't take that appointment. We're not ready."

"I disagree. I think we're totally ready. With everything we've been through, we know each other exceptionally well."

She argued her case. "I think we need more time to prepare."

"Our marriage seems real, Allison. We've fooled everyone around us, and we're going to fool the officer who interviews us, too. We've got nothing to worry about."

"I'm scared." Of living the rest of her life without him, she thought, of losing him.

"It'll be okay." He set his coffee on the table and came over to her. Behind him, the rising sun seeped through the glass doors, casting a graceful gold glow. "We can do this."

She blew out a shaky breath. She was a bundle of nerves. "What time is the appointment tomorrow?"

"Ten o'clock. If the officer approves us, he or she will stamp your passport. The stamp acts as a green card and will last thirty days, until your actual green card arrives in the mail."

"You just said *if* the officer approves us."

"I was just repeating what the notification said," he told her. "But even if they don't approve us on the spot, they probably wouldn't deny us outright, either. They'd take more time to review our case, and if they still aren't satisfied, they'd schedule us for another interview with their fraud unit."

"That sounds daunting."

"Mostly they'll be looking for inconsistencies in our stories. But we can work up some makeshift questions tonight and test each other. It might help you relax."

"Thank you. I'd like that." The outcome of the interview was out of their control. They could only do their best. But either way, she still loved Rand the way a wife should. In her heart, their marriage was genuine. She just needed to convince him that they should stay together.

He said, "It helps that we speak the same language, are around the same age and share the same spiritual beliefs. We have all of that in our favor. Our chemistry should help us, too, how obvious our attraction to each other is."

She nodded. "You're right. No one could deny that."

"Are you less scared now?"

Of the interview, yes. Of their marriage ending, no. But she said, "I'm feeling better about it."

"Good." He smoothed a strand of her hair, tucking it behind her ear.

She noticed that his tie was skewed, so she reached out to straighten it for him. Then she realized how easily they did those types of things for each other, how natural it was for them.

She lifted her gaze. "Will you kiss me?" He always kissed her before he left for work, but she wanted to be extra certain that he did it this morning.

"Of course." He slipped his arms around her waist, brought her body next to his and slanted his mouth over hers.

She savored the warmth between them and returned his kiss, as deeply and romantically as the situation would allow. She couldn't lure him off to bed. With their trip to Ireland, he'd already missed too much work as it was.

After they separated, she said, "Thank you again for helping me through my family crisis."

"I'm glad I got to meet them in person. They're such wonderful people. I hate that we're deceiving them, though. It's even worse now that I got so close to them. I hate how we're deceiving my grandmother, too. But at least my brother can say 'I told you so' to me after you and I part ways."

"I don't want to talk about that. It's not a good thing to think about so close to our interview." Nor did she feel guilty about their deception anymore. Now that her love for him had turned real, she wasn't lying to anyone.

Except for Rand, she thought miserably. Sooner or later she would have to tell him the truth. She would have to admit that she loved him. But for now, she kept quiet.

Keeping her heart all bottled up.

The following morning, Allison and Rand arrived at the local USCIS office thirty minutes early and waited in a small lobby for their names to be called. He was in business attire, and she wore a conservatively stylish skirt ensemble. She'd done her hair and makeup with an elegant touch, befitting a woman of her new social standing. Rand was a well-known millionaire. She couldn't come to the interview looking like a farm girl. But she wished that a casual top and blue jeans would have been acceptable. Being so stiff and formal was making her antsy.

They brought a packet of required documents with them, along with anything else they could think of that helped prove the validity of their marriage and the closeness of their relationship. Rand was prepared to show the interviewer his social media accounts, as well as the gossip blogs that had featured AliRan. By now, Rand was being referred to as a former play-boy and no one was suggesting anymore that Allison should run from him. She couldn't agree more.

Last night they'd spent hours quizzing each other with probable questions. They'd scored 100 percent on their makeshift tests and could only hope they did as well in the real interview.

Rand's USCIS friend wouldn't be present. Nor had he advised them in any way. All he'd done was help speed up the process. As it turned out, he didn't even work in this office. When Allison asked Rand more about him this morning, she discovered that he was an executive at the main location in Washington, DC, and was an old fraternity brother of Rand's.

Allison hadn't even gone to university. Would their interviewer think that was a red flag?

She dismissed the thought. Their levels of educa-tion didn't make them an unsuitable match. Nothing did, in her opinion. She wanted to be Rand's wife forever.

Finally, their names were called and they were directed to a windowless room down the hall, where the interview began.

The immigrant official, a middle-aged woman named Maria Martinez, interviewed them together and separately. She didn't take her position lightly. She videotaped each session and asked scores of questions. As intense as it was, Allison could tell the interview was based on more than just questions and answers. Officer Martinez analyzed their body language, too.

When it was over, she stamped Allison's passport. Their marriage was deemed bona fide, their application approved.

Once they were free to leave, they left the building and proceeded to Rand's Porsche.

He said, "I'd never been so nervous in all my life. That was way harder than I thought it was going to be, especially when she separated us."

"That part concerned me, too." But they'd obviously done everything right.

He opened her car door. "Do you want to stop for a celebratory lunch? Maybe the Tex-Mex and margaritas we never got from before?"

Allison shook her head. "I'd rather just go home. I'm not very hungry right now." She still had to figure out how to stop the divorce.

"Then I can wait, too." He got behind the wheel.

She glanced over at him. "We're still going to need to be careful over these next thirty days."

He fired up the engine. "What do you mean?"

"We can't do anything to raise suspicion. We're going to have to keep living together."

"I wasn't planning on doing anything drastic."

She relaxed a little. That gave her thirty days to win him over. Thirty days of doing what? she asked herself. Of living the same lie, of pretending nothing had changed?

No, she thought. *No.* If she was going win Rand over, then she had to tell to him how she felt. She had to admit that she loved him. She didn't want the next thirty days to be based on anything except the truth.

Allison made up her mind to do it today, just as soon as they got home. She couldn't embark on an important discussion while they were riding in the car. She needed to be in a soothing environment, where there wouldn't be any distractions.

"Do you want to change into some comfy clothes and sit on the patio when we get home?" she asked. "I could use some fresh air."

"Sure. That sounds nice. Then we can go to lunch later."

She nodded, even if food was the last thing on her mind. For now, all Alison could think about was exposing her heart.

To the man who'd become her everything.

Twelve

"Why are you looking at me like that?" Rand asked Allison, as they settled onto the patio. Now that they were outside, she was behaving strangely.

She stammered, "I just…there's just…something I need to tell you."

He prodded her to say whatever was on her mind. "What is it? What's going on?"

"I love you, Rand." Her voice went horribly, terribly scratchy. "I fell in love with you."

Good God, he thought. His worst fear had just come true, and he couldn't seem to respond. He couldn't do anything but sit there, white knuckling the arms of his chair.

"I'm sorry if this is freaking you out," she said.

Oh, yeah. He was freaked out, all right. He glanced

past her and caught sight of her fairy gardens on the other side of the patio. If he could ask the fairies to undo the spell she was under, he would. But he knew that wouldn't work.

Rand returned his gaze to hers. He needed to convince her of the mistake she was making by loving him, persuading her to see him for who he really was. "When we were in Ireland, I sensed that you were getting too attached to me. I even started comparing myself to Rich, wondering if I was as bad as he was for preying on your feelings."

She moved her chair closer to his. "You're nothing like him. You're kind and decent and heroic."

"I'm far from heroic." And he didn't feel very kind and decent, either. "I'm not the guy in the book you're going to write. You can't turn me into him."

"But what if you're already becoming him on your own?"

"You're just being idealistic." He was the wrong man for her, the wrong husband, and he knew better than to prolong the agony.

"I tried not to fall for you." She fidgeted with the hem of her buttery-yellow T-shirt, pulling at a loose thread. "So help me I did. I've been fighting my feelings for you since the night you told me about your grandfather."

"The same night you tried to rewrite my grandparents' story and give them a happy ending? Real life doesn't work that way, Allison. You can't erase the past for them, and you can't conjure up a future for you and me, either." He revealed his truth to her.

"When we were in the church in Ireland, I had a wavering moment of wondering what staying with you would be like, of renewing our vows there. But I knew it wasn't meant to be. I knew you'd be better off without me."

"So you're making this big noble sacrifice by letting me go? Wouldn't it be easier to just try to make it work?"

"I don't know how to do that. I wasn't raised like you. I wasn't taught how to be a loving, caring partner. I didn't have a family who set that sort of example. My mother loved my father and look what happened to her. He divorced her and two years later, she got sick and died."

She blew out a sigh. "We're not your parents, Rand."

"All right, then what about my grandparents? At least Lottie was smart enough to walk away from Eduardo. She knew that loving a playboy like him was a mistake. And you should know the same thing about me."

"But you're not the playboy type anymore," she insisted.

"Says who? The gossip blogs? We duped them, Allison. We duped everyone. And now you're buying into the fiction we created, too."

"Maybe you're the one who can't see reality from make-believe," she said. "Maybe you're not the wilding you always thought you were. Maybe deep down, there's always been a loving, caring partner clamoring to get out."

Frustrated with her romance-stricken ways, he dragged a hand through his hair. "You don't know what you're talking about."

"I know how thoughtful you were from the beginning, agreeing to ask for my father's blessing to marry me. How many playboys would do that? And how many would insist that he wanted to make the ring he gave his wife mean something? Or be eager about seeing her in her wedding dress? You've done things from the start that identified you in ways neither of us even considered at the time."

"And now they're a big deal? Now that you love me?" he demanded.

"Everything that's ever happened between us matters now. You could have let me go to Ireland alone. You didn't have to take that trip with me. You didn't have to get close to my family or light candles with me. And you especially didn't have to wonder what renewing our vows would be like. Do you know how major it was for you to be having those sorts of thoughts?"

"And do you know how major it was for me to decide against it?" he retorted. "That was a defining moment for me. The moment I knew I had to get our marriage to end sooner. That's why I called my friend from the USCIS and prodded him to keep hurrying things along."

She flinched. "You wanted to be rid of me?"

"I wanted to stop this from happening." He made a grand gesture, referring to her feelings for him. "I don't know how to accept your love. I don't know what to do with it." He searched her wounded gaze, wishing he could kiss and hold her and be the man she wanted him to be. "I'm so sorry. The last thing I ever wanted to do was hurt you."

Her voice hitched. "So there's no chance for us?"

"Between a marriage-minded woman like you and a confirmed bachelor like me? Not that I can see."

She squeezed her eyes shut, and suddenly he wanted to reel his "confirmed bachelor" remark back, to say that he didn't mean it. That he wanted to spend the rest of his life with her. But he was scared of making that kind of commitment. Terrified, he thought, of falling in love with her, too.

Allison opened her eyes, and they stared awkwardly at each other, pain and discomfort zigzagging between them. She glanced away, and he suspected that she was suppressing the urge to cry, trying to seem stronger than she was.

"I'm so sorry," he said again. "I'm so damned sorry."

"You don't have to keep apologizing. You never promised me that we were going to stay together. I just wanted to believe it was possible."

But it wasn't, he thought. In his screwed-up family, love never panned out. So why would it be any different for him? Allison deserved someone who understood love, who wasn't afraid of it. When Rand was on the farm and immersed in her homeland, he'd gotten caught up in the idea of it being real, of it feeling authentic. But this was getting way more real than he'd bargained for. He didn't like having emotions he couldn't escape from.

Allison stood and held on to the back of her chair. "I'm going to pack an overnight bag and head off to my apartment in Dallas. After that, I'll make plans to get the rest of my belongings and return to Ireland."

He started. "You're going to go home? And give up your green card?"

She tightened her hold on the chair. "Staying in America doesn't make sense anymore."

Hating himself for being such a miserable coward, Rand got to his feet. He hadn't just broken her heart; he'd crushed her lifelong dream of living in the States, too. He'd taken her natural sweetness, her innocence, all of the qualities he'd chosen for her to become his wife and mangled them to bits.

"I can drive you to your apartment," he said, trying to stop her from going off alone.

She shook her head. "I'd rather that you didn't. I'd also prefer that you weren't here when I come back for the rest of my things. I'll let you know what day it'll be."

"So we're never going to see each other again?"

"I think it would be easier if we make a clean break." She moved forward as if she were going to hug him goodbye, but then she pulled back, protecting herself from getting too close. "Be well, Rand. Be happy."

"You, too." He went numb inside, feeling as if a part of him was dying. The part she loved, he thought. The husband she so desperately wanted him to be.

He stayed in the yard while she packed her overnight bag and arranged for an Uber. After she was gone, he returned to his big empty house.

Missing her already.

Allison entered her apartment feeling horribly alone and trying not to cry. If she broke down in a puddle of tears, she feared the pain would only get worse. Already she hurt so badly, her bones ached from it.

She'd meant everything she'd said to Rand about what a wonderful husband he'd turned out to be, about how attentive he'd been to her. But he'd spurned her belief in him.

She didn't want to go back to Ireland, but she didn't know what else to do. Living in Texas would never be the same, not without Rand.

She sank onto her sofa and curled up into a ball. Every moment they'd spent together was turning like a pinwheel in her mind. She couldn't envision her life without him.

If he could just see himself through her eyes, he would know that she was right, that they were meant to be together.

Allison was still going to write her novel and make the hero a man like Rand. Except in the book, he was going to fall desperately in love with the heroine. He was going to believe in her, in himself, in them as a couple.

Her fantasy Rand. Her dream husband.

The tears she'd been banking began to fall—hard,

sobbing, racking tears, burning their way down her cheeks.

She got the maddening urge to call Rand, to hear his voice, but she didn't do it. She stayed on the sofa, crying for what she'd lost.

When the sogginess became too much, she went into the bathroom to get some tissues. She blew her nose until it was dry and chafed. Then, catching her tormented reflection in the mirror, she splashed water onto her face.

From there, she returned to the main room and found her way onto the patio, needing a breath of air.

She'd told Rand that she was going to arrange to get the rest of her belongings. But she wasn't going take the fairy gardens back to Ireland with her. She was going to leave them at Rand's house, so the tiny sprites could watch over him.

A gift to the man she loved.

If only the fairies could have swept her and Rand into a supernatural realm for all eternity. At least then they would still be together, frozen in time and married forever.

Rand couldn't stay home by himself. He was about ready to climb the walls, so he shot his brother a text and asked if he could stop by.

When he arrived, Trey was waiting for him in the garage and tinkering around on his workbench. He took one look at Rand and handed him a longneck from a nearby mini fridge.

Rand twisted the cap and took a swig. But he

quickly set it aside. A cold beer wasn't going to help. Nothing would.

"What's going on?" his brother asked. "What's wrong?"

Rand got right to the crux of it. "Allison left me. She went back to Dallas and soon she'll be going back to Ireland." He waited a beat before he added, "I screwed up my marriage, just like you said I would. I hurt her, bro. I broke her heart."

Trey frowned at him, a scowl of instant disapproval. But that was what Rand needed. It was part of the reason he came here. He wanted his brother to confirm his crappy character.

"What did you do, exactly? How did you hurt her?"

Rand gave him a condensed version. "After we got the approval for her green card today, she told me how wonderful I was, and I told her I wasn't cut out to be her husband."

Trey leaned against the workbench, grilling him, asking another probing question. "And why did you do that?"

"Because she thinks I'm better than I am. Because if we stay together, I'll never be able to live up to her expectations."

"But according to her, it sounds as if you already are."

Rand blinked. "Since when did you become so supportive of my marriage? You're the one who told me from the beginning that I wasn't husband material."

"Yeah, but I must have been wrong. I mean, look

at you. You're missing your wife so much, you can hardly see straight."

"Of course I miss her, but that isn't the point."

Trey made a confused face. "So what is the point? That she thinks you're the greatest guy on earth? Isn't that how it's supposed to be?"

"Yeah, but it's complicated." Rand couldn't blow the whistle on his phony marriage. He and Allison had agreed to keep that secret to their graves.

"You still love her, don't you? Because when you first came here to say that you were getting married, you kept saying how much you loved her."

Once again, Rand couldn't admit that he'd lied. But it didn't matter anyway. By now, there was no denying it. He knew that he loved Allison as passionately as she loved him. If he didn't, he wouldn't be feeling as if his heart had been ripped clean out of his chest. "Yes, I love her." He paused to come to grips with his admission, with accepting it. "I totally do."

Trey went silent, but so did Rand. His pulse was beating a mile a minute.

A few seconds later, Trey said, "You need to fix this."

"You're right, I do." He needed to figure things out. "Thanks for listening, for being here for me, but I should go."

"Don't mess it up any more than you already have."

"Yeah, I know." Rand needed to get his shit together. But damn, he'd never been in love before, either.

Their visit ended, and Rand drove straight to Dallas. He stopped at a park in Allison's neighborhood, just to keep himself close to her.

He exited the car and walked along the grass. When he came to a duck pond, he watched the birds float along the water. They looked so peaceful, content with where they belonged.

But Rand wasn't. He'd never been so lonely.

He thought about how amazing it was to have a wife who believed in him, who loved him, who felt safe and warm in his arms. Crazy thing was, she made him feel that way, too, even when he was too damn stubborn to realize it.

But he wasn't too hardheaded to know it now.

Love wasn't something to be feared and neither was commitment. They were gifts life had to offer, and so was the sanctity of marriage.

Allison had been perfect for him all along: sweet and funny and spunky, loving, sexy and supportive. Everything a man should cherish. She was his dream girl, the living, breathing fantasy he didn't even know he had. And now he wanted to settle down with her, to give her his heart, to raise a family, to be the husband she needed. But would she forgive him for the pain he'd caused her? Would she allow him to retract the hurtful things he'd said to her?

God, but he hoped so.

When the doorbell chimed, Allison ignored it. It could be someone selling something, she supposed. Or it could be the lady next door searching for her cat. On occasion, the friendly old feline jumped over the fence and slept on Allison's patio furniture. But she hadn't seen the cat today, and she couldn't bear to see anyone else, either.

She wasn't even supposed to be here herself. If she hadn't told Rand that she loved him, she would still be at his house with him. But that wouldn't have solved anything. She just would have been living a lie.

The doorbell chimed again. But once again, she didn't answer it. She needed to be alone in her misery. Not that anyone, aside from Rand, knew she was miserable.

What if it was him at the door? What if he was here?

To do what? she asked herself. Rehash the same conversation they'd had earlier, with him apologizing for not being able to return her feelings? As much as she loved him, she couldn't bear to go through that again.

Still, she took a chance and peered through the peephole. Sakes alive, but it was him.

Forcing herself to be brave, she undid the latch and opened the door. They stared at each other, gazes locked.

"Look what I've done to you," he said.

She assumed he meant her ragged appearance. He looked disheveled, too, but nothing marred his handsomeness, at least not to her.

She defended her person. "I just had a good cry, that's all." A horrible, life-will-never-be-the-same breakdown, she thought.

She gestured for him to come inside, and they

stared at each other all over again. She hated how much smaller her apartment seemed, dwarfed by his big, broad-shouldered body. He was achingly close to her.

Too, too close.

"I'm so sorry," he said, reaching out to touch her cheek. "I'm so sorry I hurt you."

She flinched and stepped away from him, his apology drumming in her ears. "Please don't do that."

"Am I too late?" A fearful expression clouded his eyes. "Have you stopped loving me?" He thumped a hand against his heart. "Because I love you, Allison."

She went dizzy, her mind spinning in all sorts of directions. Was this really happening? Had he really said that? "You love me?"

"Yes." He closed the gap between them, taking both of her hands in his. "It scared me at first, thinking that I might be falling in love with you. But I'm not afraid anymore. I want to share my life with you, to have kids with you, to do everything real married people do."

"This feels like a dream." But it wasn't. The man she loved, the man who loved her, wasn't a figment of her imagination. The hands that held hers were strong and solid, flesh and bone.

"Will you marry me a second time? Will you return to Ireland with me next year on our anniversary and have the ceremony your family wants us to have?"

She nodded. "I'd marry you a million times more."

She fell into his arms, and they held each other.

He kissed her, his mouth warm and tender against her own. Nothing had ever tasted so good or seemed so right.

After they separated and she caught her breath, he asked, "Do you have a piece of paper and a pen I can use?"

"Yes, of course. But what for?"

"I want to write something down for you."

She couldn't begin to guess what he was up to, but she would soon find out. She went over to her stationery drawer and retrieved a felt-tip pen and a small lined sheet of paper, tearing it from a notepad. "Will these do?"

"They're perfect."

He put pen to paper. But it only took him a matter of seconds. He folded the note and gave it to her.

She eagerly opened it. Along with today's date and his signature, the letters *IOU* were written on it. "I don't understand. What do you owe me?"

"I'm going to write you a poem, like the ones you used to write to your fantasy husband. I can't guarantee how long it'll take me or how good it'll be. I'm not much of a writer. But I want us to have a tangible connection to that time in your life, and that'll be my way of doing it."

Allison could have melted like a teenager at his feet. No doubt about it, he was the hero she'd dreamed about since she was a girl. He absolutely, positively was.

"I need you," she said. Here and now and naked

beside her, she thought. "Will you lie down with me? Will you hold me and touch me?"

He took her hand in his. "You know I will. I need you just as much."

She led him to her bed, and they removed their clothes. The tears she'd cried were gone now. In their place were warmth and happiness.

They turned down the covers and slid beneath them. She luxuriated in the masculine beauty of his body, in the familiarity of it. He whispered in her ear, telling her that he loved her, and hearing him say those three little words thrilled her to the marrow of her bones. She repeated them to him and felt the same wondrous thrill of saying them.

There was no actual penetration. But they made it work anyway, pleasuring each other with hands and mouths and being wildly creative. She didn't have a supply of condoms at her apartment. He hadn't brought protection with him, either. But he had love on his mind when he'd arrived at her door, not sex.

She adored him even more for that. There was nothing sexier than a man who was thinking about love. Nothing more perfect than knowing you were part of his soul.

Hours later Allison went home with Rand, marveling at his determination to share his life with her. He opened the safe in his bedroom and tore up the prenuptial agreement she'd signed, tossing it in the air and making confetti out of it.

She smiled at his boyish enthusiasm, the shredded document fluttering around them. "You're being crazy."

"Yeah, but it's a good kind of crazy." He returned her playful smile. "I want everything I have to belong to you, with no barriers between us. Speaking of which, we need to get rid of the doors between our rooms and make this one big master suite."

Allison nodded her approval. There was nothing better than being happily married, than knowing her joy in Texas was just beginning. "I think I'd like to try my hand at driving the American way, too."

He swung her into his arms. "You can do anything you want."

She squealed as he spun her around, and when his stomach growled, they both laughed. "Maybe I better fix us something to eat."

"That's probably a good idea. I haven't had anything since breakfast. I doubt you have, either."

"I was too emotional to eat. But I'm famished now. How does chicken and dumplings sound?"

"That works for me. I can help, if you want. You can teach me to cook."

"Sure. That'll be fun." She envisioned him years from now, with their children toddling around. "Then you can cook for me on Mother's Day, you and our adorable, green-eyed kids."

"Yeah, but how funny would it be if they ended up with blue or brown eyes?"

"That's a possibility. We both have blue and brown eyes in our family histories." She rocked in his arms. "Our life together is going to be amazing."

"It already is." He released his hold on her, and they went downstairs to the kitchen to start the meal.

Just as she prepared to gather the ingredients, his cell rang. She got an immediate sense of foreboding. "The last time we got interrupted by a phone call, it was bad news."

"Hopefully this is something good." He checked the screen. "It's Will."

She held her breath. Was there information about Rich or did they have an update on Megan's brother Jason?

Allison stood back while Rand talked to Will. Since she could only hear one side of the conversation, she tried not to jump to any conclusions. She waited for Rand to tell her what was going on.

After the call ended, he came over to her and said, "The test results from the ashes came in. They don't belong to Rich. He wasn't the person who died in the plane crash."

Her chest went tight. "Then who did?"

"The authorities don't know. All they know is that the ashes are male human remains."

"So Rich faked his own death? And put someone else's ashes in his place?"

"That's the assumption. But wherever that bastard is, he better never come anywhere near you again. If he does, I'll kill him myself."

"I appreciate you wanting to protect me, but I'll be fine." Allison assured her husband not to worry. "There's no reason for Rich to ever try to see me again. He took my money and that's all he ever really wanted from me."

Rand blew out a breath. "I just hope they catch him."

"Me, too." Rich was a sociopath who needed to be stopped, a rotten-to-the-core man Allison would just as soon forget ever existed. "Did Will mention Jason? Is there any word from him?"

He shook his head. "Jason still hasn't returned Will's calls. Megan hasn't heard from her brother, either. And neither has Jason's daughter, at least not since he first sent her those sporadic emails. It's disturbing, though, how closely Jason appears to be tied to this since he's the one who mailed the urn to Megan to begin with, saying that the ashes belonged to Will."

Allison had never met Jason. But she prayed that he hadn't aligned himself with Rich. She could only imagine how heartbreaking that would be to Will and Megan and the rest of Jason's family. Or worse yet, if he'd come into harm's way. "So there wasn't any positive news?"

"Actually, there was." Rand graced her with a smile. "Will's brother got married yesterday."

"Jesse and Jillian had their wedding? I heard they were engaged." She'd even thought about them on the night of the TCC fund-raiser.

"They tied the knot at the Ace in the Hole. It was an intimate family wedding. Jillian's little daughter, Mackenzie, was the flower girl. Will said she looked cute as a button."

"I'll bet she did." Mackenzie was the toddler

Rich had fathered, the same child Jesse Navarro had claimed as his own when he'd fallen in love with the girl's mother. "They're going to make a wonderful family."

"Just like us."

Rand kissed her, and Allison closed her eyes, savoring the moment. Even with the bad things that had happened in Royal, good things were unfolding, too, she thought, as he deepened the kiss and made her sigh.

Very good things.

* * * * *

Don't miss a single installment of the
Texas Cattleman's Club: The Impostor.
Will the scandal of the century lead to
love for these rich ranchers?

THE RANCHER'S BABY by
New York Times *bestselling author Maisey Yates.*

RICH RANCHER'S REDEMPTION
by USA TODAY *bestselling author Maureen Child.*

A CONVENIENT TEXAS WEDDING
by Sheri WhiteFeather.

EXPECTING A SCANDAL by Joanne Rock.

REUNITED...WITH BABY
by USA TODAY *bestselling author Sara Orwig.*

THE NANNY PROPOSAL by Joss Wood.

SECRET TWINS FOR THE TEXAN
by Karen Booth.

LONE STAR SECRETS by Cat Schield.

***

If you're on Twitter, tell us what you think of
Harlequin Desire! #harlequindesire

*Notorious playboy Nolan Madaris is determined
to escape his great-grandmother's famous
matchmaking schemes, but Ivy Chapman, the
woman his great-grandmother has picked out for
him, is nothing like he expects—and she's got her
own proposal for how to get their meddling
families off their backs and out of their love lives!*

*Read on for a sneak peek of
BEST LAID PLANS,*
the latest in New York Times *bestselling author
Brenda Jackson's*
MADARIS FAMILY SAGA!

Prologue

Christmas Day

Nolan Madaris III took a sip of his beer while standing on the balcony of his condo. Leaning against the rail, he had a breathtaking view of the exclusive fifteen-story Madaris Building that was surrounded by a cluster of upscale shops, restaurants and a beautiful jogging park with a huge man-made pond. The condos where he lived were right across from the water.

The entire complex, including the condos, had been architecturally designed, engineered and constructed by the Madaris Construction Company that was owned by his cousins Blade and Slade. For the holidays, the Madaris Building and the surrounding shops, restaurants and jogging park were beautifully decorated with colorful, bright lights. It was hard to believe a new year was just a week away.

When Nolan had arrived home from his cousin Lee's wedding, he hadn't bothered to remove his tuxedo. Instead he'd headed straight for the refrigerator, grabbed a beer and proceeded to the balcony for a bit of mental relaxation. But all his mind could do was recall the moment his ninetysomething-year-old great-grandmother, Felicia Laverne Madaris, had finally cornered him at the reception that evening. She was a notorious matchmaker, and he'd been avoiding her all night. Her success rate was too astounding to suit him—and she had calmly warned him that he was next.

He was just as determined not to be.

Nolan, his brother, Corbin, and his cousins Reese and Lee had all been born within a fifteen-month period. They were as close as brothers and had been thick as thieves while growing up. Mama Laverne swore her goal was to marry them all off before she took her last breath. They all told her that wouldn't happen, but then the next thing they knew, Reese had married Kenna and today Lee married Carly.

What bothered Nolan more than anything about his great-grandmother setting her schemes on him was that she of all people knew what he'd gone through with Andrea Dunmire. Specifically, the hurt, pain and humiliation she had caused him. Yes, it had been years ago and he had gotten over it, but there were some things you didn't forget. A woman ripping your heart out of your chest was one of them.

His cell phone rang. Recognizing the ringtone, he pulled it out of his pocket and answered, "Yes, Corbin?"

"Hey, man, I just wanted to check on you. We saw you tear out of here like the devil himself was after you. It's Christmas and we thought you would stay the night at Whispering Pines and continue to party like the rest of us."

Whispering Pines was their uncle Jake's ranch. Nolan took another sip of his beer before saying, "I couldn't stay knowing Mama Laverne is already plotting my downfall. You wouldn't believe what she told me."

"We weren't standing far away and heard."

Nolan shook his head in frustration. "So now all of you know that Mama Laverne's friend's granddaughter is the woman she's picked out for me."

"Yes, and we got a name. Reese and I overheard Mama Laverne tell Aunt Marilyn that your future wife's name is Ivy Chapman."

"Like hell the woman is my future wife." And Nolan couldn't care less about her name. He'd never met her and didn't intend to. "All this time I thought Mama Laverne was plotting to marry the woman's granddaughter off to Lee. She set me up real good."

Corbin didn't say anything and Nolan was glad because for the moment he needed the silence. It didn't matter to him one iota that so far every one of his cousins whose wives had been selected by his great-grandmother were madly in love with their spouses and saw her actions as a blessing and not a curse.

What mattered was that she should not have interfered in the process. And what bothered him more than anything was knowing that he was next on her list. He didn't want her to find him a wife. When and if he was ready for marriage, he was certainly capable of finding one on his own.

"You've come up with a plan?" Corbin interrupted Nolan's thoughts to ask.

Nolan thought of the diabolical plan his cousin Lee had put in place to counteract their great-grandmother's shenanigans and guaranteed to outsmart Mama Laverne for sure. However, in the end, Lee's plan had backfired.

"No, why waste my time planning anything? I simply refuse to play the games Mama Laverne is intent on playing. What I'm going to do is ignore her foolishness and enjoy my life as the newest eligible Madaris bachelor."

He could say that since, at thirty-four, he was ten months older than Corbin, who would be next on their great-grandmother's hit list. "By the time I make my rounds, there won't be a single woman living in Houston who won't know I'm not marriage material," Nolan added.

Corbin chuckled. "That sounds like a plan to me."

"Not a plan, just stating my intentions. I refuse to let Mama Laverne shove a wife that I don't want down my throat just because she thinks she can and that she should."

After ending the call with his brother, Nolan swallowed the last of his beer. Like he'd told Corbin, he didn't have a plan and wouldn't waste time coming up with one. What he intended to do was to have fun; as much fun as any single man could possibly have.

A huge smile touched his lips as he left the balcony. Walking into his condo, he headed for his bedroom. Quickly removing the tux, he changed into a pair of slacks and a pullover sweater. The night was still young and there was no reason for him not to go out and celebrate the holiday.

As he moved toward his front door, he started humming "Jingle Bells." *Let the fun begin.*

One

Fifteen months later...

Nolan clicked off his mobile phone, satisfied with the call he'd just ended with Lee about his cousin's newest hotel, the Grand MD Paris. Construction of the huge mega-structure had begun three weeks ago. Already it was being touted by the media as the hotel of the future, and Nolan would have to agree.

Due to the hotel's intricate design and elaborate formation, the estimated completion time was two years. You couldn't rush grandeur, and by the time the doors opened, the Grand MD Paris would set itself apart as one of the most luxurious hotels in the world.

This would be the third hotel Lee and his business partner, DeAngelo Di Meglio, had built. First there had been the Grand MD Dubai, and after such astounding success with that hotel, the pair had opened the Grand MD Vegas. Since both hotels had been doing extremely well financially, a decision was made to build a third hotel in Paris. The Grand MD Paris would use state-of-the-art technology while maintaining the rich architectural designs Paris was known for.

Slade, the architect in the Madaris family, had designed all three Grand MD hotels. Nolan would have to say that Slade's design of the Paris hotel was nothing short of a masterpiece. Slade had made sure that no Grand MD hotel looked the same and that each had its own unique architecture and appeal. Slade's twin, Blade, was the structural engineer and had spent the last six months in Paris making sure the groundwork was laid before work on the hotel began. There had been surveys that needed to be completed, soil samples to analyze, as well as a tight construction schedule if they were to meet the deadline for a grand opening two years from now. And knowing Lee and DeAngelo like he did, Nolan expected the Grand MD Paris to open its doors on time and to a fanfare of the likes of a presidential inauguration.

After getting a master's graduate degree at MIT, Nolan had begun working for Chenault Electronics at their Chicago office. Chenault Electronics was considered one of the top ten electronics companies in the world. The owner, Nicholas Chenault, was a family friend, had taken Nolan under his wing and had not only been his boss but his mentor, as well.

After working for Chenault for eight years, Nolan had returned to Houston three years ago to start his own company, Madaris Innovations.

Nolan's company would provide all the electronic and technology work for the Grand MD Paris; some would be the first of its kind anywhere. All high-tech and trend changing. It would be Nolan's first project of this caliber and he appreciated Lee and DeAngelo for giving him the opportunity. Lee and his wife, Carly, spent most of their time in Paris now. Since DeAngelo and his wife, Peyton, were expecting their first child four months from now, DeAngelo had decreased his travel schedule somewhat.

Nolan also appreciated Nicholas for agreeing to partner with him on the project. Chenault Electronics would be bringing years of experience and know-how to the table and Nolan welcomed Nicholas's skill and knowledge.

Nolan had enjoyed the two weeks he'd spent in Paris. He would have to go back a number of times this year for more meetings and he looked forward to doing so, since Paris was one of his favorite places to visit. There was a real possibility that he might have to live there while his electronic equipment was scheduled to be installed.

Nolan leaned back in his chair. In a way, he regretted returning to Houston. Before leaving, he had done everything in his power to become the life of every party, and his reputation as Houston's number one playboy had been cemented. In some circles, he'd been pegged as Houston's One-Night Stander. Now that he was back, that role had to be rekindled, but if he was honest with himself, he wasn't looking forward to the nights of mindless, emotionless sex with women whose names he barely remembered. He only hoped that Ivy Chapman, her grandmother and his great-grandmother were getting the message—he had no intentions of settling down anytime soon. At least not in the next twenty-five years or so.

He rubbed a hand down his face, thinking that while he wouldn't admit to it, he was discovering that living the life of a playboy wasn't all that it was cracked up to be. Most of his dates were one-night stands. There were times he would spend a week with the same woman, and occasionally someone would make it a month, but he didn't want to give these women the wrong idea about the possibility of a future together. He was probably going to have to change his phone number due to the number of messages from women wanting a callback. Women expecting a callback. Women he barely remembered from one sexual encounter to the next. Jeez.

Nolan wondered how his cousins Clayton and Blade, the ones who'd been known as die-hard womanizers in the family before they'd settled down to marry, had managed it all. Clayton had had such an active sex life that he'd owned a case of condoms that he'd kept in his closet. Nolan knew that tidbit was more fact than fiction, since he'd seen the case after Clayton had passed it on to Blade when Clayton had gotten married.

Blade hadn't passed the box on to anyone when

he'd married. Not only had he used up the case he'd gotten from Clayton, but he'd gone through a case of his own. Somehow Clayton and Blade had not only managed to handle the playboy life, but each claimed they'd enjoyed doing so immensely at the time.

Nolan, on the other hand, was finding the life of a Casanova pretty damn taxing and way too demanding. And it wasn't even deterring Ivy Chapman.

Nolan picked up the envelope on top of the stack on his desk. He knew what it was and who it had come from. He recalled getting the first one six months ago and he had received several more since then. He wondered why Ivy Chapman was still sending him these little personal notes when he refused to acknowledge them. All the notes said the same thing... *Nolan, I would love to meet you. Call me so it can be arranged. Here is my number...*

Nolan didn't give a royal flip what her phone number was, since he had no intentions of calling her, regardless of the fact that his matchmaking great-grandmother fully expected him to do so. He would continue to ignore Miss Chapman and any correspondence she sent him. He refused to give in to his great-grandmother's matchmaking shenanigans.

He tossed the envelope aside and picked up his cell phone to call his family and let them know he was back. He had slept off jet lag most of yesterday and hadn't talked to anyone other than his cousin Reese and his brother, Corbin. Reese and his wife, Kenna, were expecting their first baby in June and everyone was excited. For years, Reese and Kenna, who'd met in college, had claimed they were nothing but best friends. However, the family had known better and figured one day the couple would reach the same conclusion. Mama Laverne bragged that they were just another one of her success stories.

Nolan ended the call with his parents, stood and walked over to the window to look out. Like most of his relatives, he leased space in the Madaris Building. His electronics company was across the hall from Madaris Explorations, owned by his older cousin Dex.

He loved Houston in March, but it always brought out dicey weather. You had some warm days, but there were days when winter refused to fade into the background while spring tried emerging. He was ready for warmer days and couldn't wait to spend time at the cottage he'd purchased on Tiki Island, a village in Galveston, last year. He'd hired Ron Siskin, a property manager, to handle the leasing of the cottage whenever he wasn't using it. So far it had turned out to be not only a great investment but also a getaway place whenever he needed a break from the demands of his job, life itself and, yes, of course, the women who were becoming more demanding by the hour.

The buzzer sounded and he walked back over to his desk. "Yes, Marlene?" Marlene was an older woman in her sixties who'd worked for him since he started the company three years ago. A retired administrative assistant for an insurance agent, Marlene had decided to come out of retirement when she'd gotten bored. She was good at what she did and helped to keep the office running when he was in or out of it.

"There's a woman here to see you, Mr. Madaris. She doesn't have an appointment and says it's important."

Nolan frowned, glancing at his watch. It's wasn't even ten in the morning. Who would show up at his office without an appointment and at this hour? There were a number of family members who worked in the Madaris Building. Obviously, it wasn't one of them; otherwise Marlene would have said so. "Who is she?"

"A Miss Ivy Chapman."

He guessed she was tired of sending notes that went unanswered. Hadn't she heard around town what a scoundrel he was? The last man any woman should be interested in? So what was she doing here?

There was only one way to find out. If she needed to know why he hadn't responded, that he could certainly tell her. She could stop sending him those notes or else he would take her actions as a form of harassment. He had no problem telling her in no uncertain terms that he was not interested in pursuing an affair with her, regardless of the fact that his great-grandmother and her grandmother wanted it to be so.

"Send her in, Marlene."

"Yes, Mr. Madaris."

Nolan had eased into his jacket and straightened his tie before his office door swung open. The first thing he saw was a huge bouquet of flowers that was bigger than the person carrying them. Why was the woman bringing him flowers? Did she honestly think a huge bouquet of flowers would work when her cute little notes hadn't?

He couldn't see the woman's face behind the huge vase of flowers, and without saying a word, not even so much as a good morning, she plopped the monstrosity onto his desk with a loud thump. It was a wonder the vase hadn't cracked. Hell, maybe it had. He could just imagine water spilling all over his desk.

Nolan looked from the flowers that were taking up entirely too much space on his desk to the woman who'd unceremoniously placed them there. He was not prepared for the beauty of the soft brown eyes behind a pair of thick-rimmed glasses or the perfect roundness of her face and the creamy cocoa coloring of her complexion. And he couldn't miss the fullness of her lips that were pursed tight in anger.

"I'm only going to warn you but this once, Nolan Madaris. Do not send me any more flowers. Doing so won't change a thing. I've decided to come tell you personally, the same thing I've repeatedly told your great-grandmother and my grandmother. There is no way I'd ever become involved with you. No way. Ever."

Her words shocked him to the point that he could only stand there and stare at her. She crossed her arms over her chest and stared back. "Well?" she asked in a voice filled with annoyance when he continued to stare at her and say nothing. "Do I make myself clear?"

Finding his voice, Nolan said, "You most certainly

do. However, there's a problem and I consider it a major one."

Those beautiful eyes were razor-sharp and directed at him. "And just what problem is that?"

Now it was he who turned a cutting gaze on her. "I never sent you any flowers. Today or ever."

*Find out if Nolan Madaris has finally
met his match in
BEST LAID PLANS
by* New York Times *bestselling author
Brenda Jackson, available March 2018
wherever HQN Books and ebooks are sold.*

www.Harlequin.com

Available April 3, 2018

#2581 CLAIM ME, COWBOY

Copper Ridge • by Maisey Yates

Wanted: fake fiancée for a wealthy rancher to teach his father not to play matchmaker. Benefits: your own suite in a rustic mansion and money to secure your baby's future. Rules: deny all sizzling sexual attraction and don't fall in love!

#2582 EXPECTING A SCANDAL

Texas Cattleman's Club: The Impostor • by Joanne Rock

Wealthy trauma surgeon Vaughn Chambers spends his days saving lives and his nights riding the ranch. But when it comes to healing his own heart, he finds solace only in the arms of Abigail Stewart, who's pregnant with another man's baby...

#2583 UPSTAIRS DOWNSTAIRS BABY

Billionaires and Babies • by Cat Schield

Single mom Claire Robbins knows her boss is expected to marry well. Taking up with the housekeeper is just not done—especially if her past catches up to her. Falling for Linc would be the ultimate scandal. But she's never been good at resisting temptation...

#2584 THE LOVE CHILD

Alaskan Oil Barons • by Catherine Mann

When reclusive billionaire rancher Trystan Mikkelson is thrust into the limelight, he needs a media makeover! Image consultant Isabeau Waters guarantees she can turn him into the face of his family's empire. But one night of passion leads to pregnancy, and it could cost them everything.

#2585 THE TEXAN'S WEDDING ESCAPE

Heart of Stone • by Charlene Sands

Rancher Cooper Stone owes the Abbott family a huge debt...and he's been tasked with stopping Lauren Abbott from marrying the wrong man! But how can Lauren trust her feelings when she learns her time with Cooper is a setup?

#2586 HIS BEST FRIEND'S SISTER

First Family of Rodeo • by Sarah M. Anderson

Family scandal chases expectant mother Renee from New York City to Texas. But when rodeo and oil tycoon Oliver, her brother's best friend, agrees to hide her in his Dallas penthouse, sparks fly. Will her scandal ruin him, too?

Get 2 Free Books,
Plus 2 Free Gifts—
just for trying the Reader Service!

HARLEQUIN *Desire*

HD17R3

Joshua Grayson looked out the window of his office and did
not feel the kind of calm he ought to feel.

He'd moved back to Copper Ridge six months ago from
Seattle, happily trading in a man-made, rectangular skyline
for the natural curve of the mountains.

But right now he doubted anything would decrease the
tension he was feeling from dealing with the fallout of his
father's ridiculous ad. Another attempt by the old man to
make Joshua live the life his father wanted him to.

The only kind of life his father considered successful: a
wife, children.

He couldn't understand why Joshua didn't want the same.

No. That kind of life was for another man, one with
another past and another future. It was not for Joshua. And
that was why he was going to teach his father a lesson.

He wasn't responsible for the ad in a national paper
asking for a wife, till death do them part. But an unsuitable,
temporary wife? Yes. That had been his ad.

He was going to win the game. Once and for all. And the woman he hoped would be his trump card was on her way.

The doorbell rang and he stood up behind his desk. She was here. And she was—he checked his watch—late.

A half smile curved his lips.

Perfect.

He took the stairs two at a time. He was impatient to meet his temporary bride. Impatient to get this plan started so it could end.

He strode across the entryway and jerked the door open. And froze.

The woman standing on his porch was small. And young, just as he'd expected, but… She wore no makeup, which made her look like a damned teenager. Her features were fine and pointed; her dark brown hair hung lank beneath a ragged beanie that looked like it was in the process of unraveling while it sat on her head.

He didn't bother to linger over the rest of the details—her threadbare sweater with too-long sleeves, her tragic skinny jeans—because he was stopped, immobilized really, by the tiny bundle in her arms.

A baby.

His prospective bride had come with a baby.

Well, hell.

Don't miss
CLAIM ME, COWBOY
by New York Times *bestselling author Maisey Yates,*
*part of her **COPPER RIDGE** series!*

Available April 2018 wherever
Harlequin® Desire books and ebooks are sold.

www.Harlequin.com

LOVE
Harlequin
romance?

Join our Harlequin community to share your thoughts and connect with other romance readers!

Be the first to find out about promotions, news, and exclusive content!

Sign up for the Harlequin e-newsletter and download a free book from any series at **www.TryHarlequin.com**

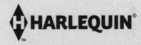